BOOK ONE OF THE AFTER THE PULSE SERIES

HOMESTEAD

L. DOUGLAS HOGAN

COPYRIGHTS

Cover by Deranged Doctor Designs
Edited by Pauline Nolet Editing Services
Interior art by James B. Hogan
Copyright © 2018 Disgruntled Dystopian Publications
L. Douglas Hogan

PREFACE

I've spent the last twenty-five years doing jobs that a rational person wouldn't do, i.e., military, law enforcement, maximum-security environments, etc. I bring this up in my preface because it has a direct effect on my writing style. Everything I write is an influence from someone, something, or someplace that has affected me in some way.

In February 2015, I wrote *Oath Takers* because of the political divisions and ideologies that were and still are destroying this country from the inside out.

In May 2015, I published my first work of fiction, Tyrant book one. It was written because of my passion and love of country. The same passion that went into *Oath Takers* spilled over into the Tyrant series. It reflects the best and worst of American ideologies. What would happen if the majority controlled the rights of the minority? Take a look around! It's already happening. When did this country become a democracy? When did the will of the many take control of the rights of the few? The short answer is, we fell asleep at the wheel and it was a slow casual drifting that our parents led us into, and we, in turn, are leading our children into. It's the slow steady progressive movement from a constitutional republic, where the rights of the individual are unique to that person, to a democratic rights-controlled voting procedure, where your rights are determined by the winning party.

Why am I saying these things in a preface? Because I want to illustrate to the reader the passion behind my words. When I write a post-apoc work of fiction, it's done for the purpose of waking Americans up to the reality of what can and will happen to America if we don't awaken from our slumber. In my twenty-five years, I've seen the best and the worst of humanity. I've seen its love and its hate. Its division and its solidarity.

The book you now hold in your hands is not a politically motivated book. It's not fact-based fiction like the Tyrant series was. No, this book is a work of fiction that showcases the human spirit when it reaches new levels of depravity. Despite the ugliness of people when they're trying to survive, there is still a hope that lingers in the human heart. It's never too far gone to change or to come back from the brink of despotism. There will always be strong people leading weak people, and there's nothing we can do to stop it from happening. What we can do is make sure the people whom we are following remain accountable to the people doing the following.

Homestead does not get into the political events that lead up to the grid-down condition. Instead, it focuses on the human element that is affected by the political events that lead to the condition. We are the elements that must survive the coming apocalypse. We are the people who must make the toughest decisions of them all. The power of life and death are in the tongue, and we must live with the choices we make and the leading of the people we choose to follow. We cannot let smooth-speaking men beguile us with their words, or follow after the man with the biggest armory. We must work together to maintain our freedoms. Our liberty is what makes us American. We become something else when we think we can control our fellow man, whether by gun, the voting booth, or word and deed.

I sincerely hope you enjoy this series. Please be kind and leave a review when you have finished reading. If you're interested in receiving updates and notifications of future releases, you can register for my newsletter at:
www.ldouglashogan.com/newsletter.html

Sincerely,

L. Douglas Hogan

"Everyone has a plan until they get punched in the mouth." - Mike Tyson

MEMORIES FROM THE GLADE – THE BODY OF OLIVER HECHT

The Glade
Mitchell Homestead
August 16th

Dirt flew from a deep rectangular hole in the earth – a man stood in its base, his eyes squinted with each thrust of his shovel into the hard layer of clay. The deeper he went, the more difficult the digging became. Sweat dripped down the man's brow as he stopped to catch his breath. A wipe of his forehead with the leather gloves he was wearing offered momentary comfort. No sooner than he had caught a line of sweat, another would seep from his forehead. The lines on his brow were full of mud, as were the shallow crow's-feet that stretched from the corners of his eyes. Darrick had shot a stranger, and the man's body rested just behind his shoulder on the edge of the grave he was preparing.

I think this is deep enough, he thought.

Darrick rested his back against the dirt wall. The plan was to catch his breath before climbing out. He was a fit thirty-five-year-old man native to Georgia, but hailed from Tennessee. He had married Tonya ten years ago. She gave birth to Andy nine months later. The Pulse was two years ago. Everything changed after that.

Darrick's older brother, Jimmie, lived with their dad, James, whom Jimmie was named after, on his homestead one state down on the southeast coast of Georgia. It wasn't exactly a valuable piece of real estate, but the ground was fertile and the home was well hidden behind the rolling plains and forests. The property had a garden that had been maintained by the Mitchell family for generations. The temperature was a warm and bearable 50 to 60 degrees Fahrenheit in January and February. It was the perfect bugout location. Immediately after the Pulse, Darrick had grabbed Tonya and Andy and headed there on foot against his wife's wishes. She had wanted to locate her family in New York. Her incessant requests to head east diminished in time. It took a lot of killing before she accepted the fact that the cities and rural areas were in far worse condition than the countryside. That didn't stop her from worrying about her kin or bringing them up in conversation to Darrick on occasion. They were, after all, blood, and blood was worth fighting for.

Darrick tossed his shovel out of the pit and jumped up to the edge of the earth, hoisting himself up and out of the grave. The man he shot was about fifty years of age and had been brandishing nothing but an empty pistol holster. He had cracker crumbs in his left pocket and a few loose rounds in his right. In his back pocket was a skinny wallet with nothing more than a picture of what might have been his daughter and wife. And a photo identification card listing him as Oliver Hecht, from a town in southeast Georgia. The man was numbered among others he'd recently buried – most likely murderers of dozens of men, women, and children; at least that was what Darrick kept trying to convince himself of. Perhaps this man was just a wanderer, maybe a looter or even a killer; there was no way to know. Darrick's mindset? It was the stranger or Darrick and his family. The old ways were gone. The new rule of thumb was to kill or be killed. This man couldn't be allowed to discover their homestead. If they were discovered, others might come. In the end, they would certainly die. That was why it had to remain secret. His family's survival depended upon it.

There was no formal ceremony, no kind words, poems, or prayers. Darrick rolled the man over toward the grave and watched him fall in. It was a hard fall. He never grew used to the sound bodies made when they fell limp from a height of six feet. He wished things were different, but they weren't. This was the new world. It was a cold harsh reality. Turn off the feelings. Shut out the emotion. Separate yourself from any emotional response that could be exploited or cause you to hesitate. That was Darrick's new mantra. It had worked until this day.

Darrick looked around, stood up, and thrust his shovel into the pile of dirt, scooping as much as he could manage. Looking down at the man one last time, the stranger's eyes were wide open and facing the noon sun. His killer dumped the first scoopful onto the man's face, burying his hazy-colored eyes in permanent darkness.

Tired and exhausted from several hours' work, he grabbed the fingers of his sweaty leather work gloves and pulled them off one at a time. He looked at the fresh mound of earth.

I didn't even know the man. I had to. I had to kill him. I had to kill him for family… because of Jimmie.

His brother, Jimmie – well, that was a sad story too.

BLOOD ON THE STAIRS

Mitchell Homestead

A few months ago

Knock, knock, knock, Jimmie heard from the kitchen. He always had a shotgun and rifle that he kept within arm's reach. He grabbed the shotgun and looked back at his wife, Carissa. "Are you expecting company, hon?"

"No," she said, running for the bedroom. She was just doing what she was expected to. Jimmie always told her to run for his dad's bedroom. After the Pulse, he'd lifted some planks in the floor under his dad's bed and made a temporary hiding spot between them and the downstairs ceiling. He threw a pistol in there, too, for added protection. There wasn't a lot of space, but it was enough to hide.

Jimmie darted for the front room. His only neighbors were two married couples who lived several miles apart. Both of their homes were well out of view of each other, even from the tops of the rolling hills. He didn't bother them, and they didn't bother him. That was just the way things were. One of the families, the Berts, had been friends with elder James Mitchell, Jimmie's father, years ago. James had fallen ill and eventually forgot about the Berts. Since then, Jimmie and his wife had been taking care of the homestead and his ailing father. Elder Mitchell was difficult to care for. There was no good contingency plan that didn't involve high risk for Jimmie and Carissa. He was stubborn, loud, and had aggressive tendencies.

With his shotgun at point, Jimmie made his way through the front room and positioned himself where he could see through the curtains at the intruders. At first all he saw was a shadow, the shape of an adult male. Jimmie pointed his shotgun at the shape of the man and prepared to pull the trigger.

Nobody's got no reason to be here, but to take what ain't theirs, Jimmie thought.

He was about to shoot the gun and blow a hole through the window to save himself, his wife, and his father. He could always patch the door up with boards, but he couldn't bear to lose his family. The trigger had about a four-pound pull weight to it, and he had already squeezed three pounds of pressure from it when he heard a familiar voice.

"Jimmie! It's Darrick. Are you in there?"

Jimmie's heart dropped. He released the trigger.

Oh God, I almost shot Darrick.

He threw the curtain open to see his not-so-little brother, Darrick, standing on the porch. His wife, Tonya, and their son, Andy, were away in the distance. Darrick knew that approaching the front door was a dangerous risk, so he'd kept them back.

Jimmie was glad to see them. He ran for the door and pulled it open. They embraced for the first time in some years.

"Pudge! I feared the worst," Jimmie confessed, calling Darrick by his childhood nickname. "Carissa," Jimmie shouted, "it's my brother, Darrick, and his family. It's okay. You can come out."

"It's been a long road, Jimmie. We're tired and hungry. Do you have a bite to eat? We're starving."

"Well, get your family in here. I have some vittles. We can all eat together."

"Where's Dad?"

"Dad's been sick, Pudge."

"Sick? Sick how?" Darrick asked, stepping into the house with Tonya and Andy. No sooner than they were in the front room and the door was closed, Carissa and elder James Mitchell stepped into the front room.

James looked at Darrick and his family. "Who in Sam's hell are you?" he challenged.

"Funny, Pop," Darrick quipped.

"Get the hell out of my home," James barked, heading for the closet, where he searched for his rifle.

Darrick stretched his arms out to protect Tonya and Andy. Each of them stayed behind Darrick, who was deeply confused at this point.

"Come on, Dad. That's Pudge. Your youngest son. Let's go finish reading the paper," Jimmie pleaded, grabbing his dad by the shoulders and steering him to the kitchen area. "Have a seat, Pudge. I'll be back to explain everything in a second."

Darrick was beginning to realize how sick his dad was. He didn't want to admit to the fact that his dad didn't recognize his own son.

Darrick turned around and took a knee to speak with Andy. "How about you go outside and chase some of them chickens?" he whispered. Darrick would sometimes whisper things to Andy, making him believe that he was allowing him to do something forbidden. Andy grabbed the door handle and ran outside. Jimmie stepped back into the front room and looked at Darrick. "Pudge, why haven't you been in touch?"

"Come on, Jimmie. Don't pretend we haven't been barely surviving out there."

"I mean before that. Before the Pulse. Where have you been?"

"Adulting, I guess. You know I've never been a good communicator. We've had our own issues."

Jimmie looked at Tonya. "Hey, sis," he said, giving her a hug and a kiss on the cheek.

"Hi, Jimmie," she responded. Tonya was a quiet woman. She was most vocal during her time alone with Darrick or when she had some important issue on her mind. It was in those moments she tended to blurt out whatever she was thinking.

Jimmie did a half-turn and saw Carissa entering the room and invited her into the salutations. "Carissa, this is my brother, Darrick; his wife, Tonya; and –" realizing Andy wasn't anywhere to be seen, he looked around for his nephew.

"Where'd Andy go?" he asked.

"I sent him outside to play," Darrick answered.

Concerned about the homestead being discovered, Jimmie asked the most obvious question. "Were you careful to make sure nobody followed you here?"

"Of course. Have you had many visitors?"

"There was a couple who passed through here two weeks back. They were headed east," Jimmie said, looking at Tonya. "It was a man and his wife. They asked for some supplies, but all I was willing to spare was a couple of jars of canned tomatoes. I'm reluctant to give more. Especially not knowing from day to day how Dad's going to be. I have to feed three."

"If you don't mind my asking," Tonya said, "what happened to Emily?" She was curious what had become of Jimmie's first wife.

"You don't have to answer that, Jimmie," Darrick interrupted, looking at Tonya. "That was rude," he whispered to her.

"It's okay, Pudge. Emily left me right after the Pulse. She was hell-bent on hooking back up with her mom and dad. I wanted a family of my own. If she hadn't left me, I wouldn't have found Carissa."

At first Tonya felt ashamed for blurting out the question, but she felt vindicated that the story had a good ending. Tonya had spent the past several weeks nagging Darrick about heading to New York to hook up with her family. Darrick wouldn't budge on it. It was a sour spot in their relationship. For the time being, she was happy to be with Darrick, other than the excruciating pain in her abdomen that she was bearing from her sickness.

Darrick, on the other hand, pounced on the moment. "So you're agreeing with me that a woman's place is by her man's side?"

"Absolutely," Jimmie answered. "A woman who has joined a man in holy matrimony shouldn't be hesitant to stay with her man wherever he goes. I tried to talk Emily out of leaving. I doubt she made it all the way to Texas in these conditions. It's just –"

"Too dangerous?" Darrick answered, finishing Jimmie's sentence.

Jimmie could sense that there was a rub between Darrick and Tonya over the subject matter. Tonya was squirming like she had something to add, but she held her peace.

Jimmie felt inclined to change the subject. His sister-in-law was wandering over to the window to check on Andy. "He should be fine over there in the chicken coop," he reassured them. "As long as he stays below the ridge. Now, let's get you guys fed."

"I'm going to take a look around the property," Tonya said, opening the door to go outside.

"No problem, just be sure not to travel out beyond the first set of hills. I make a habit of keeping this place a secret. The more we expose ourselves to the horizon, the more chances that some band of miscreants will find us. If you don't mind, make sure Andy knows that."

"Sure thing," she answered, heading out the door.

"I'll come show you around," Carissa interjected before stepping outside with Tonya.

"Join me in the kitchen, Pudge," Jimmie invited.

"I wish you would quit calling me that. I haven't been overweight since grade school."

"Oh, come on! Grandpa called you that and you loved it."

"Yeah, well, Grandpa's dead and you're not him."

"Dad called you that, too."

"Yeah, until I knew what it meant. He always got a laugh outta calling me that. I guess it's extra funny when the person you're name-calling doesn't get it."

"Anyway, I have no intention of breaking with family tradition. Grandpa called you Pudge, Dad called you Pudge, and –"

"Dad has old-timer's, doesn't he?" Darrick asked, interrupting Jimmie's lightheartedness.

"Alzheimer's kicked in before the Pulse. At first, I thought it was just old age. He would forget his truck keys and sit in the cab for several minutes trying to figure out why it wasn't running. After that, he forgot

AFTER THE PULSE I BOOK 1 I HOMESTEAD

that Mom passed away. He still walks around the house calling out *Tina*. I knew he needed special care, but with the new healthcare system and the economic drain, I just couldn't afford it. His insurance refused to pay out, too. They said that I wasn't listed as power of attorney or his legal guardian, so… it just didn't work out. I coulda used your help, Pudge."

"That's not fair, Jimmie. You know I had problems of my own. Andy's autistic, and Tonya was diagnosed with ovarian cancer."

"Dear God, I didn't know."

"Yeah, see! You're just as guilty for not staying in touch."

"The phone line ran both ways, Pudge."

For a moment, Darrick felt as if he were a teenager again. Arguing with his big brother about this or that. He took in a big breath and let it out in a sigh. "It's good to be home, Jimmie."

"It's good to have you home."

For a few seconds there was an awkward silence between them. Darrick sent his mind back in time to try to dig up some positive memory that he and Jimmie shared. He came up short, so he broke the silence with the first thing that wasn't completely negative. "Hey, remember those firecrackers I hid in the closet of my old bedroom?"

"That's a random question. Yeah, I remember. Why?"

"I don't know. I was thinking of maybe popping them off this Fourth. I figured the hills and woods would displace the sound so outsiders wouldn't know where it was coming from."

"Well, they're still up there, but I don't think that's a good idea. I left that closet alone. It was just about the only thing I had left of you besides those old toys."

"Yeah, you're probably right," Darrick said, happy that the awkward silence was over.

Jimmie dug through the kitchen closet, which was right behind the back door. Finding what he was looking for, he grabbed a jar of pickled eggs that had his initials etched onto the lid. He set it in the middle of the kitchen table and said, "Dinner is served."

"Pickled eggs?" Darrick asked rhetorically.

"Times are tough, Pudge. If it wasn't the apocalypse and the wind wasn't blowing too hard, we could BBQ some chicken, but I'm thinking canned goods are great, given the situation at hand."

The last thing Jimmie wanted was for the presence of their homestead to rise into the air in the form of a sweet-smelling cookout. The smoke would be dangerous itself, but add the smell of cooking meat and you'd be inviting trouble.

"What's up with the initials on the canned goods?" Darrick asked.

"That's just something I started doing after the Pulse. I figured if anybody ransacks the house while we're away, we can at least identify the culprits if they have my initials."

"Smart idea," he said.

Darrick opened the back door of his childhood home and yelled, "Come and get it."

"Coming," Andy called. Carissa and Tonya were right behind him.

Darrick caught a glimpse of the old red barn that their great-grandpa had built generations ago. It looked like it was being dismantled from the top down.

"What's up with Grandpa's barn, Jimmie?"

"I figured it was too tall. I didn't like the way it crested the hilltops – plus, we needed firewood."

Tonya, Andy, and Carissa stepped in, and the vinegar smell of pickled eggs caught their attention. Most of them sat down around the tiny kitchen table and used their forks to dig out a high-protein meal.

"What do you remember about farming, Pudge?" Jimmie asked.

"Not much. You know I've been spoiled by city life. Gatlinburg was good to me. I had no reason to farm."

"Yeah, other than forgetting your roots and the required skillset for the end of days," Jimmie bantered.

Darrick glared at Jimmie and shook his head with a half-cocked smile on his face. Jimmie had more questions for his little brother, but they would have to wait.

"So how long do you plan on staying?" Jimmie asked, getting right to the point.

"I'm home," Darrick answered.

"I'm glad to hear it. There's a few things you need to know, then. Me and Carissa have a rule you should know about."

"Oh?"

"When you leave, the door gets locked. When you come back, it's *knock, knock, pause, knock.* Get it?"

"That's easy enough to remember. Anything else?"

"Always let us know where you're going and how long you plan to be gone. We have to communicate. Not communicating properly can cause some major issues, but you already know about that, Mr. Military Man," Jimmie joked.

Darrick had a lot he wanted to teach them, too. Security-related issues. But he didn't want to seem too intrusive too fast, so he would wait for the right moment.

The table was small, so Jimmie stood and let his tired brother sit. He couldn't help but wonder at his little brother Darrick. Looking upon him, he was a little disheveled, by normal standards, but looked amazing considering what he'd been through. With Jimmie's curiosity at an all-time high, he felt compelled to address the pink elephant. "So what happened to you out there, Pudge?"

Darrick dropped his fork and looked at his son, Andy. He wasn't eating his egg. He was just playing with it.

"Andy, Uncle Jimmie might have some of my old Hot Wheels cars upstairs."

Andy's eyes lit up. He loved cars. Mostly because they could drive in his imagination. He thought that was cool.

Carissa saw that Darrick was trying to redirect Andy, so she said, "Andy, come with me and I'll show you where they are."

Andy dropped what he was doing and followed Carissa.

"She's seems like a nice lady, Jimmie."

"She's great."

"Andy's gone. What do you want to know? I'm sure you have a few questions burning inside you."

"What's it like out there?"

"The cities and suburbs are burning. People are dying or dead. Any and all survivors have only gotten this far because they're willing to do anything necessary to survive. Out there, you're either a predator or the prey. There's no gray area. If you're not willing to kill, then you'll get killed. We had a few close calls."

"Did you have to kill anybody?"

Darrick looked down at his egg and pushed it around on his plate before he answered, "A few times." Darrick was worried that he would be judged by his brother. Their dad had raised them Catholic and always taught them that murderers go to hell. One of Darrick's great fears was that Jimmie was going to hold that over his head. He didn't.

"I'm sure they had it coming," Jimmie answered, looking at Darrick and Tonya.

"They did," Tonya answered, trying to reassure her husband.

Jimmie saw the conflict and worry in Darrick's eyes. He wanted to reassure him as Tonya had. "Killin' and murder's not the same thing, Pudge."

Darrick looked up at his brother and nodded his head in affirmation just before returning to his well-earned pickled egg.

Months later
August 13th

There was a grove of apple trees on the second hill north of the Mitchell homestead. Every fall Jimmie would head out and walk along the base of the hill to collect apples that fell from the trees and rolled down the grassy knoll. There was a reason Jimmie did it this way. He knew that exposing himself to the hill lines could jeopardize his safety.

He, his father, and Carissa had remained secure all these months because he was careful to abide by this strict rule. Picking fresh apples would require him to walk along the tops of the hills, exposing himself. He only did that at night, in absolute darkness. Jimmie knew that in the daylight hours, waiting for them to fall was the most prudent thing to do. He explained this to Darrick, Tonya, and Andy on several occasions. Darrick took it as a matter of fact, but Andy had difficulty grasping such things.

One day, Andy was chasing the chickens when his tummy started to rumble. His mouth was dry and gritty from the dirt he kicked up in the coop. He remembered hearing about the apple trees on the north side of the homestead. With an overwhelming desire to moisten his tongue with the taste of a juicy freshly picked sweet apple, he headed for the hills.

***

Homesteading wasn't as easy as Darrick remembered. This vegetable plant needs loose soil, and that fruit plant needs to be packed tightly. We plant the seeds from this plant and the shoots from that plant. There were so many things to remember. The August harvest consisted of digging up the sweet potatoes and plucking the cantaloupe. On the homestead, nothing went to waste. After the humans ate the cantaloupe, the chickens pecked away at the inner portions of the rinds. The seeds were dried out and saved for the next harvest. The sweet potato roots were also saved and stored in the house, where it was cool and dry. The shoots were saved for replanting after the last frost. Jimmie had spent the last several months teaching Darrick the tricks of homesteading. There was a lot to know.

Darrick returned the favor by showing Jimmie, Tonya, and Carissa how to maintain sight alignment/sight picture with the iron sights of the hunting rifles and how to pack a day bag. "You put the heavy items on the bottom," Darrick would teach, "and the items that you think you might use most frequently go somewhere handy and accessible." Darrick put three packs together in all and spent time equipping them with survival items that they might need in a get-out-quick situation.

On this particular August day, Darrick was working in the garden on his hands and knees.

This is rough on the ol' back, he thought occasionally as he dug away in the vegetable beds.

Jimmie looked out the window and checked on his brother from time to time, making himself available in case Darrick needed help.

"He's catching on pretty good," Jimmie said to Tonya, who was sitting at the table with Carissa.

"It must be tough having to be so mindful of your dad and tend to things around the property," she replied.

"Carissa helps with Dad quite a bit, but sometimes he gets violent. It's hard not knowing which Dad we're going to see from time to time."

"What do you mean by that?"

"Dad was aggressive with us when we were kids. I think the stress is what killed Mom. I know it's the reason why Pudge always ran off to be with his friends. I had to put up with Dad on my own. It made me tough, and for a long time I was bitter towards Pudge. But later in life, when I was wiser, I realized why Pudge did the things he did. It was his way of fighting back. I was never strong enough to protect him."

"You both turned out pretty good."

Carissa stood up and walked around behind Jimmie and rubbed his back. "I keep this one straight," she joked.

"Look at him now." Jimmie nodded towards the window. Both women walked over to the window to look outside at Darrick as his hands got dirty in the garden. "When he was a kid, he would run off with his friends instead of tending to his chores. One day the police came knocking on our door. They had Darrick in the backseat of the cruiser. They said they caught him pulling street signs out of the county roads. It's a good thing nobody got killed, they said. Pudge got the beating of his life after the cops left. I never told him, but I got it the next day for telling Dad he went too rough on Pudge."

"I never knew you guys had it like that," Tonya said, looking at Jimmie with sad eyes.

"It's nothing he would talk about. All he did in high school was fight. After detention he would come home and get the belt until he was old enough to punch. Dad slowed down after that. I guess his fists would get sore. I'm not saying Darrick didn't need some discipline. I'm just saying it made him tough. After high school, he ran off and didn't come back for years. He joined the Marines and didn't tell us." Jimmie turned to look at Tonya. "He didn't even send us an invitation to your wedding."

Tonya turned away, feeling somewhat ashamed, and said, "He said he didn't want to see his dad. He was afraid that inviting even you would mean that he'd have to face him, too. I tried to be the peacemaker, but he wouldn't budge on it." After saying that, she changed the tone of the conversation by asking, "Have you two done anything to tie the knot?"

Jimmie grabbed Carissa by the hand and pulled her around to the front of him. "It's the apocalypse. We've not seen a judge or preacher since the Pulse, so we figure we're married in the eyes of God. We made our own vows. Someday, we'd like a child."

Without comment, Tonya's eyes started darting around the room.

"What's the matter?" Jimmie asked.

"Where's Andy?"

"I thought he was outside with Pudge."

All three of them shot out the door. Tonya called over toward the garden, "Hon, have you seen Andy?"

"I thought he was with you," he answered, standing up to look towards the chicken coop. "He's not out here."

Jimmie and Carissa headed back into the house and started calling for Andy. Darrick and Tonya ran around the yard in search of their son. He was nowhere to be seen.

Jimmie ran out of the two-story farmhouse. "He's not in the house, Pudge. Check the orchard."

Darrick started running north towards the apple orchard. As soon as he was on top of the first set of rolling hills, he saw the silhouettes of three men. He immediately dropped before he could be seen, and weighed all of his options.

Do I have time to go get help? Should I warn the others or just approach the strangers?

Realizing he hadn't seen Andy, he low crawled into a position that offered him a visual over everything that was taking place on the next hill. The three men were with his son, and they were armed with rifles and backpacks.

Back at the house, Jimmie could see Darrick in the distance. He was lying on his belly, facing north. He knew there was a problem. "Stay here," he commanded Tonya and Carissa. He ran to the basement and grabbed four rifles. They were clumsy in his hands as he ran up the stairs. He handed one to Tonya and the other to Carissa. "I hope Pudge showed you how to handle yourself. Find a place to hide, but be ready in case we need backup," he said, heading out the back door in a hurry.

Darrick was watching two of the three men pick fresh apples from the trees when Jimmie came up from behind him and took a place by his side, handing him a rifle.

"How many are there?" Jimmie asked.

"I count three. Two of them aren't doing much but picking apples. The third one appears to be having a conversation with Andy."

"What's the plan?"

"Well, do you recognize any of those guys?"

"No. They look like they might be traveling, judging by the size of those packs."

"I think we need to hit them quick. Those packs can be cumbersome and hard to maneuver in. The problem is that Andy's in the way."

Andy was busy talking to the stranger when he abruptly pointed towards the house. Jimmie and Darrick both ducked their heads as the man Andy was talking to looked to where he was pointing. The immediate concern was that Andy had just given away the position of their homestead.

"We need to move our position," Darrick said.

"I agree."

Both men crawled backwards a few feet and then stood up and ran west until they selected another hilltop to watch the strangers from. By the time they had taken up their new positions, Andy was on his way back home with a mouthful of apple.

"Where'd they go?" Jimmie asked.

Jimmie and Darrick couldn't see them.

"I don't know. Go get Andy and take him back to the house. I'm going to recon the area and see if I can spot them and make sure they left," Darrick said.

"You got it." Jimmie headed back down the hill and disappeared out of Darrick's sight.

Okay, hotshot. What now? Darrick thought as he scanned the area. When he saw that Andy was safely with his uncle Jimmie, he ran to the orchard and took a position on his belly to once again scan the area.

There you are.

Darrick spotted the men, only there weren't three. There were two.

Where'd you go?

Darrick knew his reconnaissance mission wasn't complete. One man was still at large, only he didn't know where he was at.

Moments later

Jimmie had the family safely secured in the farmhouse. He was patiently looking and waiting for his little brother to return with news that the three men had left the property.

When Darrick came running from around one of the grassy knolls, Jimmie was elated. "Tonya! Pudge is back."

Tonya ran from her position at the front-room window and met up with Jimmie at the back door.

Darrick walked in and Tonya embraced him. "I was worried about you. Don't leave alone like that anymore."

"I'm fine, hon. But I had to make sure they left."

"Did they? Did they leave?"

Jimmie turned to face Darrick, anticipating a positive answer to the question.

"Two left. I can't say for the third."

Darrick recognized the fearful look in Tonya's eyes.

Carissa was equally fearful.

"What now?" Carissa asked.

"We can't wait for something to happen. There's a man out there, and we need to hunt him down," Darrick answered.

"Hunt him down and do what, Pudge?"

"First, we need to find out what his intentions are and why he's here."

"And if his intentions are ill?"

Darrick looked at Andy, who was playing with Darrick's childhood toys, oblivious to their conversation.

"We put him down."

"We don't *put people down*, Pudge. First, we need to find him. He could be out hunting and gathering for all we know."

"The problem is that he's hunting and gathering on our property."

"Our property?" Jimmie contended.

"Yeah, it's Dad's property, and he's not exactly in his right mind, now is he?"

"You were gone for years, Darrick. You show up nearly a year ago and suddenly things are *ours* again? That's not how it works. I was here for Dad when Mom died. I was here for Dad when he started getting sick. You were off playing soldier boy."

An awkward silence fell in the house.

Darrick knew that when Jimmie stopped calling him Pudge and called him by his legitimate name that they were fighting. Jimmie was very upset.

"Fine," Darrick answered. "We'll play it your way. We stay in here and hide, and hopefully we're not discovered."

Darrick started walking for the door.

"Where are you going?" Jimmie challenged.

"I'm going to check on the Bert homestead. Somebody has to watch out for them." Darrick opened the door and was almost out when he poked his head back in the door and said something to Jimmie in a calm voice that convicted his heart. "I wasn't *playing soldier*, Jimmie. I was overseas fighting a bloody war so the sheep back home wouldn't have to worry about wolves on their doorsteps."

With that comment, Darrick slammed the door shut.

Carissa elbowed Jimmie's ribs. "That was asinine of you."

"I mean, he's going to get us killed going off looking for a stranger. What if he starts a fight between us and... God forbid, a group bigger than us?"

There was another awkward silence, this time between him and Tonya. Carissa took notice and gave Jimmie a stern look, nodding toward Tonya.

"And for the record," Jimmie added, "I never knew Pudge was fighting in the war. He didn't write home; he didn't call home..."

"Can I go outside with Dad?" Andy interrupted.

"No, hon. It's not safe," Tonya said in a soft tone, making eye contact with Jimmie.

Even though Darrick and Tonya had only been married a little more than a decade, he'd known her since she was a teenager. The community was so small that even secrets were hard to come by. Darrick would bring her over to the house along with other friends because he knew elder Mitchell was always on his best behavior when there was company. The look Tonya was giving him said more than any words could say.

"You want me to go with Pudge to check on the Berts, but if I do, I leave you, Andy, Carissa, and Dad here alone. I ain't going to have that on my conscience if things go bad."

"If something happens to Darrick and he dies – out there alone, after you just had a fight with him – that will be on your conscience, too."

Carissa still had a rifle in hand. "We can defend ourselves against one man, James."

James was Carissa's serious name for *Jimmie*. He paid attention to her words when she used it.

"I see I'm outvoted here," he conceded. He gave Carissa a kiss on the cheek and walked past Tonya, straight out the door.

Jimmie stopped on the porch and looked around for anything out of the ordinary, like people. The coast was clear, so to speak. He stepped off towards the Berts' homestead.

Several minutes later, Darrick was moving around the countryside, taking up tactical positions anywhere he could. Every tree had something to offer. If he saw there was nothing to be concerned about, he ran for the next tree. With each rush, he would bring the buttstock of the rifle up to his cheek and scan the environment. His decision to go looking for the lone wolf was being carried out. He knew that he had to act swiftly and silently and take out the threat before it took them out. Darrick had a tactical mind, but oftentimes he would make the right decision the wrong way. Nobody would have been able to convince him that finding the stranger was a bad idea.

He was now on the opposite side of the apple orchard, facing in the direction of his dad's homestead. None of it could be seen, for the rolling hills were many. He used the elevation, when it was tactically sound to do so, to look for the intruders. The two who left alone were now long gone. The straggler was still nowhere to be seen. Darrick was starting to worry that he might not find the man. With each passing breath, he knew the threat was increasing. He felt that something bad was about to happen when suddenly he heard the sound of a gunshot coming from the south.

That's the homestead.

Darrick bolted for the house, running over every hill he knew he wasn't supposed to be cresting. Going the long way around them meant spending valuable time that he couldn't redeem.

The Berts' Homestead

Jimmie was resting against the rabbit cages on one knee. Behind him stood a sixteen-foot silo. Its mere presence indicated farm life, sustenance, and independence. It hadn't been used in years, but any would-be traveler with an inkling of curiosity would see it and check it out. The fact that it was empty mattered little. The land was ripe with gardens, rabbits, and chickens. Jimmie had to be careful approaching the Berts' front door. They hadn't seen him since long before the Pulse, and they were likely to shoot on sight. He was still several yards away from the home, and he was extremely pessimistic about the whole situation. There was no sign of Darrick, and this was where he'd said he was going.

Did he lie about going to check on the Berts? Did I miss him?

Jimmie mustered up the courage to advance towards the house. He stood and made a quick run for the front door, making sure to keep an eye on the windows of the property. The one thing that frightened him the most was the possibility of seeing the front tip of a rifle pointing in his direction.

He made it. His back rested against the side of the house, and he listened quietly for voices, but heard nothing but the breeze and a few chicken clucks. Jimmie knocked on the door, but never switched his position.

"Hello? It's Jimmie Mitchell – your neighbor. I'm looking for my brother, Darrick. Did he come this way?"

Jimmie waited for an answer, but the moment was awkwardly unpleasant. It was clear that somebody had been living here. The questions that plagued Jimmie's mind were *where are they?* and *where's Pudge?*

I can't believe I'm doing this.

Jimmie reached up to the door handle and gave it a twist and a pull. The door opened.

"Hello? This is Jimmie Mitchell, your neighbor. Is anybody home?"

Jimmie had seen enough.

If Pudge came here, he would be here, but nobody's here, so he didn't.

Jimmie's curiosity took hold, and he thought that he might as well check the backyard before leaving. He crept along against the siding until he reached the back of the house and peeked his head around. The back door was open, and old man Roy Bert was lying partially in the doorway and partially on the steps. He was dead from an apparent bullet wound to the chest. There was a fresh pool of blood beneath him. Not too far from the back door, his wife, Sue, was lying on her belly. She had a bullet hole in her back. It looked like she had been running away when she was shot. Jimmie grabbed his mouth with his free hand. This was the first time he had ever witnessed a murder scene. To say he was scared would be an understatement. He ran over to Mrs. Bert and rolled her body over. She was still warm and limber. She hadn't been dead long. Hoping she was still alive, he checked her for breathing and a pulse.

Voices!

Jimmie heard men's voices. He couldn't tell which direction they were coming from, but he was confident it was the sound of at least two males. He sat motionless, almost petrified at the thought of being discovered. He was by no means a cowardly man, but he knew the odds were stacked against him. He was untrained in the use of tactics, but knew that two against one were bad odds. Looking down at old lady Bert's body, he knew that he was facing the same end if he couldn't pull it together and make some smart moves. A few yards behind the Berts' house was a grove of trees.

If I can make it to those trees, I should be able to wait them out until it gets dark... No, I can't do that. If I wait here, Pudge may come looking for me, then we'll both be in hot water. Pudge – it's because of him I'm in this predicament. I'll hide in the trees long enough to wait them out; then I'll make a run for it. Hopefully I won't be seen.

Jimmie ran for the grove and went three or four trees deep, just far enough to keep himself concealed and still keep an eye on the happenings around the Berts' home.

Mitchell Homestead

Darrick was running for his dad's house as fast as he could. Along the way he remained aware of the possibility that the man he was secretly hunting might in fact be hunting them now. He worried about the gunshot and feared the worst. On the final stretch, Darrick could see the house, and the back door was clearly open. The storm door was blowing loosely in the breeze.

Where's Jimmie? I need Jimmie, he thought, hoping for backup.

Darrick charged in the back door, bumping into the kitchen table as he did. He stopped to compose himself and to listen for clues. The sounds of whimpering voices were heard in the front room and suddenly a cry from his wife.

"Darrick – Darrick, is that you? He has Andy!"

Darrick charged into the front room to see a man leaning against the closet door with Andy in a chokehold and a gun pointed at his head.

"Don't take another step, mister, or I'll pop his cap all over the front-room floor."

"You do it and you'll be dead," Darrick threatened.

Darrick, Carissa and Tonya were all pointing their rifles at the man. He was a scruffy-looking man in his forties with dirt clogging the pores of his skin. He was wounded, with blood dripping down his side. He had been shot by one of the women, and Darrick took notice.

All I have to do is wait him out, Darrick thought. *He can't go anywhere, and he's bleeding out.*

Darrick was hoping that Jimmie would come busting in at any second to lend a hand with the situation. It never happened.

"Back it up," the man commanded, pressing his pistol into Andy's head.

Andy let out a moan.

"Do what he says," Darrick instructed Tonya and Carissa. Not knowing where Jimmie was, he was forced to play things out.

All three of them backed up, and the man headed for the door with Andy tightly in his grasp. Darrick made a quick study of the situation and surmised that the man had more energy than he thought he would have for the amount of blood that was on the floor. Perhaps it was adrenaline; perhaps the man was adept at survival. Despite the reason, Darrick knew he could not let the man exit the house with his son in tow. He waited for his opportunity to take the stranger out.

As the man moved from the closet door to the front door, he turned his head to look and see where the handle was. That was when Darrick brought his pistol up and squeezed the trigger.

The Berts' Homestead

"There's gotta be sum'n in here to eat," one of the men said as he searched through the cabinets of the Berts' home.

"Shawn, do you really expect to find canned goods stashed away two years after the Pulse?"

"I dunno, Larry. You can't blame me for try'n. I done found food before in them there other homes of those prepper people."

"You're an idiot. Do you really think those old fogies were *prepper* types?"

"They be raise'n rabbit and chickens. That's a good indicator. At least it worked before."

Both men made their way through the house, searching for whatever they could find. They tried to keep their backpacks light, but full of the essentials. Food, fire-starting materials, alcohol, ammunition, and the like were all perfect for the taking, but the rabbits, chickens, and large amounts of fuel were not allowed to be taken. Denver wouldn't allow it.

"You best get your mind off those farm animals. You know the boss is particular about what we're allowed to take and what we're supposed to leave."

"I know, I know. Stop remind'n me."

Shawn and Larry were now standing in the back door.

Shawn took one glance out the back door and said, "Larry, wasn't she lyin' on her belly when we left 'er?"

"You tell me. You're the one who shot 'er."

Both men stood still and studied the bodies of the deceased Roy and Sue Bert. Shawn took notice that the lady he'd shot and left lying on her belly was now lying on her back. Both he and Larry moved outside, stepping over Roy's body, into the backyard.

"No, I'm sure she landed on 'er belly when I shot 'er."

"Maybe you didn't kill her and she rolled over. You know, like the way chickens flop around when you take their head off or snap their neck."

"Maybe somebody moved 'er."

Both men took their packs off and set them on the ground. They began to carefully scan the environment.

Larry jumped when Shawn suddenly yelled, "Don't move, mister!"

He looked over at Shawn and saw him pointing his rifle into the woods. A man with a blue shirt stuck out like a sore thumb. Larry brought his rifle up and joined Shawn in pointing it at the stranger. He was tall and slender with a five o'clock shadow.

"Come out where we can see you," Larry added.

Jimmie raised one of his hands and slowly lowered the rifle that was in his other hand onto the ground. He recognized the two men. They were the same two men who had been with Andy in the orchard. The one doing all the shouting with a funny twang to his voice was disheveled with a beard and mustache. It was unkempt, which wasn't uncommon after the Pulse. He had streaks of white in it, which stood out and made him easily identifiable, even from a distance. The other man had a less noticeable facial marker – a scar that ran down his face on the left side. It was about three inches long from his cheekbone to his jawline and fairly fresh.

"I don't want no trouble," Jimmie offered up with his hand in the air.

"Trouble?" Shawn asked. "You haven't seen trouble. You see that woman right there? You see her dead man in the doorway? They saw trouble. You ain't seen no trouble. But you gonna see trouble."

Shawn leaned into his rifle, but Larry said, "Wait. We might need him." He put his hand on Shawn's rifle and pushed it down from his life-taking gaze.

"Need 'im for what?"

Larry didn't answer directly. Instead, he kept his focus on the stranger in the woods.

"Where you from, stranger?" Larry asked him.

When he didn't get an immediate response, he became irate. "I ain't asking you again, mister. Now, you tell me where you came from."

If I answer honestly, they're likely to kill me, Dad, Carissa, Pudge and his family. If I answer dishonestly, how long will I be able to keep up this charade?

"I'm from a homestead three miles west of here," he lied, deciding that it was best to lead them as far away from his family as possible. "It's all gone now, so I'm out looting like you guys."

"You ever killed a man before?"

"Only for not cooperating," he answered with another lie.

Larry patted Shawn on the back. "See, I told you we could probably use him."

Shawn was still very suspicious of the stranger. He raised his rifle back up and pointed it at the man. "I don't like 'im, Larry. There's something about him that doesn't smell right," he said, with a sneered look seemingly stuck to his face.

Shawn thought for a moment then offered up another question. "Where'd you say you were from again?"

"I'm not going to say another word to you as long as that rifle is pointed in my direction."

Shawn lowered the rifle to appease the stranger. He figured he was a good enough distance away from them to get a shot off if he had to. "Kick that rifle over," Shawn commanded the stranger.

Jimmie kicked the rifle over towards the two men. There went his only chance at survival and the ability to shoot back at them.

Jimmie was trying to reason his way out of this predicament. He was having a hard time being decisive. *I need Pudge. These men are going to kill me. If I can get them close enough to the homestead and find a way to alert the family, maybe Pudge and the girls can get me out of this mess.*

"I lied. I'm really from Tennessee. I've been heading south into warmer climates for the past several months. I've killed plenty of people for food and water. Whatever I have to do to survive."

"He lied to us, Larry. We really can't trust 'im."

"You can trust me. You keep me alive and I keep you alive. We work together to survive. If I can do this by myself, I can do this with help."

I hope to God they buy this lie. I'll tell them anything they need to hear.

"Good answer," Shawn said, lowering his rifle for the second time.

"Can I have my rifle back now?"

"I think you should give it to him, Shawn."

"I think he needs to earn it first. We don't know squat about 'im. Let's see how he survives relying on us before we have to rely on him."

"Fair enough," the stranger answered.

"What's your name, mister?" Larry asked.

"Cole. My name's Cole," he answered, deceiving them yet again.

"Well, Cole… lucky for you, we're headed south, too. In case you haven't figured it out yet, this here's Shawn, and I'm Larry."

"Where's your friend?" Jimmie asked, realizing that he'd just made a mortal error in judgment.

"Who said anything about a friend?" Shawn asked, bringing his rifle back up to threaten Jimmie's life.

Jimmie had to think quicker on his feet if he was going to outsmart these two men. They didn't seem particularly intelligent, but Shawn had a nose for smelling deception and seemed a little more bloodthirsty than Larry.

"I'm talking to you, Cole. Tell me how you know about our friend? Are you Andy's dad?"

Jimmie's heart sank at hearing that. Shawn was putting the pieces together, and Jimmie worried that soon he'd be dead and his family would be soon to follow.

"I told you! I'm from Tennessee and I'm heading south. I know there's three of you because I've been hiding here for a while. I've been watching you."

"You see, Shawn," Larry said, hitting him on the arm. "If he couldn't be trusted, he coulda killed us by now."

Shawn wasn't buying the story. "How long you been watch'n us?" Shawn asked.

"Long enough to see the three of you."

Shawn shot the deceiver in the leg.

Jimmie let out a loud cry and dropped to the ground.

"Why'd you do that, Shawn?" Larry yelled.

"Think about it, you simpleton. Just because you got better speech than me don't mean you're brighter! If he was heading south, he'd know that there's more than three of us. This man's from that homestead where we saw that kid. That's the only way he'd have seen Max. They must not know about him; otherwise he wouldn't have come after us."

"Unless Max is dead and he's just scouting us out," Larry added.

A realization that they might be getting picked off one by one hit Shawn in the face like a ton of bricks.

"We need to get over there now. Grab the stranger. We might need 'im for leverage," Shawn said, taking control of the situation.

"Who died and made you boss?"

"If Max is dead, Denver'll skin both of us alive! We're supposed to stay together. Them are the rules."

Jimmie was lying on the ground, putting pressure on the bullet wound as the two argued. Every ounce of pressure he put on it to control the bleeding caused that much more pain. He could feel where the bullet stopped. There was a hard knot between his hamstring and the skin on the back of his leg.

Jimmie thought, *I need to cut an opening just over the top of the bullet so I can pull it out. It's right there. I can feel it. Problem is, I don't have a knife.*

He watched the two men as they bickered about some man named Denver, and he wondered if he would be able to make a run for it.

Not possible. This hurts too bad. I wouldn't reach the front yard before being shot dead.

Jimmie noticed the pool of blood under his leg was getting larger. Fear gripped his heart as he groped at his leg.

"Guys?" he called to them.

They stopped their bickering to look at the stranger.

"Ah, hell," Larry said.

"That's a lot of blood," Shawn replied.

The two men walked up to Jimmie just as he lay down. He was light-headed and losing consciousness.

Shawn pulled his rifle up and pointed it at Jimmie's head. Larry stopped him again by putting his hand on Shawn's rifle and pushing it down.

"We might as well finish 'im off," Shawn insisted.

"Why waste a bullet? He's bleeding out. I think you hit an artery. Give him a minute or two and save yourself a bullet."

Jimmie lost sense of what was happening. The pain in his leg abated, and his thoughts wandered back to the homestead, where he hoped Carissa was doing well. His last memory before losing consciousness was of little Pudge looking out the front-room window as his big brother, Jimmie, got on the school bus when they were children. Pudge's face would be sad as he waved goodbye. Jimmie felt guilty leaving Pudge alone with Dad, but there was nothing he could do about it. Jimmie had to leave, and Pudge had to take care of himself. The dirty glass pane of the window on the front of that old farmhouse glistened, even through the grime, because on the other side of it, Pudge was there waiting for Jimmie to look back at him every morning before he stepped onto the bus. That was his last memory. A hundred school bus pickups coalesced into one, with Pudge's sad eyes as he waved goodbye.

MEMORIES FROM THE GLADE – JIMMIE'S WATCH

The Glade
Mitchell Homestead
August 16th

Darrick's back was stiff from shoveling. He wanted to stand as tall as he could and stretch his arms into the air. He could never be too careful, so he looked about to make sure nobody was visible.

Trees. I see lots of trees, but no people.

He stretched as tall as he could. When he was done, he walked over to a separate section of the makeshift cemetery. The graves weren't that old – three in all, not counting Jimmie's or the fresh empty plot. He looked upon them and considered their lives. The significance of taking men's lives weighed heavily on his conscience.

Darrick's weight gave in at his knees as he thought about everything that had happened and everything that had befallen the homestead. He fell hard into a sitting position next to one of them. With sad eyes and a heavy heart, he looked down at it. He rested his left hand on top of the loose dirt, and he looked at his watch. It was an old Timex that had belonged to his brother, and his father before that. It had stopped working a long time ago. He wasn't sure why he wore it. A memento, maybe. It served as a distraction at best.

He turned his head back to the set of graves. Unlike the grave of his brother, these graves were unmarked. If not for the trouble they could bring, he would have strung them up by their necks. One in each tree. That wouldn't be tactically sound, so he had to bury them. He reminisced – or he tried to. He kept looking at Jimmie's watch. The more he looked at it, the more he felt torn between sorrow and rage. It was the combination of the two that edged him closer and closer to reckless and negligent behaviors. He felt obliged to do some crazy thing, but in the back of his mind, Andy and Tonya were there to anchor him. That was where he found his peace in the storm. He wanted Jimmie's watch to fuel his rage. He wanted it to direct his anger.

BLOOD ON THE FLOOR

Mitchell Homestead

August 13th

The stranger took the shot to the head, but it wasn't enough to kill him. The bullet that Darrick fired pierced the bridge of the stranger's nose and stunned him into letting go of Andy. The boy, stricken with fear and panic, ran out the door. Darrick, seeing the blood that was quickly escaping from the man's face, hesitated.

Die, just die already.

The man must not have sustained a fatal head shot, but that took a moment to analyze. The stranger used that moment to point his pistol in the direction of Darrick and pulled the trigger. Stunned, Darrick searched himself over for a bullet hole. Nothing.

The man was now facing Darrick for the first time since being shot. One of his eyes was blown completely out and was missing. The other eye was dangling from the socket. The man pulled the trigger again, but he didn't realize the slide of his pistol was already locked to the rear. His magazine was empty and he had shot his last bullet. He dropped to his knees, and Darrick ran up to him, kicking him in the head with his right knee as hard as he could. The man shot backwards onto the hardwood floor and continued to bleed and moan.

Darrick straddled the man and used his bare hands to choke out what remained of the stranger's life. He could hear the women behind him crying as the man's arms and legs struggled to gain control. It was pointless. The stranger's equilibrium was gone with his vision, and he had no sense of direction. His struggles were momentary. Darrick pressed down on the man's neck until he was lifeless.

Darrick regained his composure and stood. Looking back at the women, he asked, "Are you okay?"

Both Carissa and Tonya had lost their poise. Darrick looked them over, trying to see if they were shot. About that time, elder Mitchell came walking into the front room.

"Not now, Dad," Darrick said.

Elder Mitchell was confused. All he saw was the two women crying hysterically. He had already forgotten about the gunshot sound that drew him out of the bedroom to begin with. He ran for the coat closet to grab the shotgun, but it wasn't there, so he turned to Darrick and charged him with his bare hands. He bolted between the two women, believing that he was running to their defense.

Darrick scooped up his dad in a bear hug and carried him back to his room, where he released him and closed the door. Darrick stood against the door as his dad beat on the other side. His dad threw swear words and demands, but Darrick shut out his father and sank to the floor, keeping his weight against the door. The ladies were not yet composed. He needed them to help keep elder Mitchell in his room until things were calm and Andy was found. From his position, he heard the crying come to a stop.

"Tonya, you there?" he called out.

Carissa came walking around the corner to meet Darrick.

"I think she went looking for Andy," she said, wiping her eyes and nose on her shoulder.

"Would you mind holding Dad back while I go get Tonya and Andy?" he asked.

She nodded yes and traded positions with him. Darrick left her alone. She called out to him as he was leaving, "Jimmie went looking for you," hoping he would also find her husband. He didn't hear her voice. He was already too far gone.

Outside, Tonya was calling for Andy, and he wasn't responding. Darrick followed her calls and joined her near the chicken coop, where Andy usually played.

"Don't stray too far," Darrick told her. "There's still two more of them out there."

Darrick shot off towards the apple orchard while Tonya searched the areas closer to the house. It wasn't long before she heard the chickens' clucking pick up. She immediately headed for the coop. Now standing at the fence door, she called out, "Andy, you in there?"

There was no answer, but she knew somebody was in there because the chickens were worked up over something. With rifle still in hand, she pointed it upward and moved toward the door. She cracked it open and saw Andy hiding in the corner under a nesting box.

"Andy, it's okay, baby," she said, reaching out her hand to take his.

He shook his head no and cowered back into the corner.

"You really need to stop calling him *baby*," Darrick said, startling her. "I heard the chickens, so I came back."

"See if you can coax him out," she demanded, frustrated at his lack of empathy. Tonya stormed off toward the house.

"Hey, pal," Darrick said to Andy. "You plan on staying in there forever?"

"The bad man was going to kill me."

"That's not going to happen, son. I stopped him. He's not going to bother any of us ever again."

"I heard you shoot him. Did it kill him?"

Darrick felt uncomfortable sharing the details of the stranger's death with him, so he lied. "Yeah. It killed him."

Darrick watched Andy for some kind of reaction, but something about Andy was a little off. He was used to managing Andy's autism, but Andy had never been taken hostage before, so he really wasn't sure what mental challenges he might face having to deal with the process.

"Listen, pal – those guys who talked to you in the orchard – was he one of them?"

Andy nodded his head.

"What did they say to you? Did they mention to you how many of them there were or if they were going to visit our home?"

"The bad man didn't talk to me. He just listened. The other men asked where I lived, so I showed them."

"Did they say anything? What did they say?"

"One of the men whispered to me."

Darrick grabbed him by the shoulders. "What did they whisper to you, son?"

"Quit picking our apples."

"Where's your uncle Jimmie?"

"I don't know."

Darrick was all the more frustrated at the lack of answers. "You need to come out of there now! There's two more bad men out there, and I don't know where they're at."

Andy stood up and began making his way to the door of the coop. "Do you think they'll try to kill me again?"

"I'm not going to let anything happen to you, Mom, Aunt Carissa, Uncle Jimmie, or Papa. Do you understand?"

Andy shrugged his shoulders then jumped down out of the enclosure. As he was walking back to the house, Carissa came storming out the back door, right past Andy and into Darrick's face.

"Jimmie went looking for you, and he's not back yet!" she said with her finger pointed squarely at his forehead.

"Went looking –" Darrick cut himself short, realizing that his big brother went to the Berts' homestead. It was a lie he'd told Jimmie and the others to avoid a conflict of words so that he could find the third stranger. Now matters were worse. His son was possibly suffering from a traumatic event, his brother was missing, and a dead man was on the floor of the house.

Carissa was watching Darrick's expression, hoping to see some sign of regret or even an apology. "Well? What are you going to do about it?"

Darrick didn't apologize. He pushed past her and in doing so said, "I'm going after him."

"And what about us?"

Darrick stopped. "Lock up tight and make sure your rifles are loaded."

Tonya came out of the house to join the conversation and said, "Your dad's asleep, finally – what's going on?"

"I need to go after Jimmie. He should have been back by now."

"What about us? What about Andy and your dad?"

"Just lock everything up tight. Carissa, do you have enough hiding spaces in the house to conceal everybody?"

"No. Just the one. Your dad's going to be fully exposed if those men show up. You know there's no shutting him up until he gets tired of yelling."

"Then show Andy where the hiding place is and make sure he makes it in. The two of you will have to make do until I return. I don't know what else to do. I'm not leaving him out there. Something might have happened to him, and I aim to find out what it is."

Darrick turned to leave, and Tonya gave Carissa a stink-eye before walking away. She didn't like the attitude she presented, but she felt vindicated knowing that her husband was at least trying to correct a wrong.

The Berts' Homestead

A mile or so east, Shawn and Larry were dragging the Berts' bodies into the woods. Larry had Sue by the leg, and Shawn had Roy by the arm. Neither men afforded the deceased an ounce of respect.

Larry reached the wood line first and said, "Drop the old man and help me chuck her behind this here log."

Shawn let go of Roy's body and headed over to assist Larry by grabbing Sue's legs. Together they hoisted her into the air, saying, "One, two, three!" and let her go. Her dead remains flew limp through the air as she sailed into the woods. Before she even hit the ground, Larry was assisting Shawn by grabbing Roy's legs.

"Wait," Shawn said.

"Wait for what?"

"Should we keep'm together?"

"Why not?"

"I guess it don't matter. I just don't want no stink when Denver passes through here. You know how he is with smells 'n things."

"You're probably right. Maybe we should burn them, then?"

"There ya go! Now you're cook'n with butane!"

"What about the liar?"

"We'll fetch him out of the woods, too, I suppose."

The two men stepped into the woods and grabbed Sue's lifeless body. They dragged her out of the woods and tossed her on top of Roy's body.

Shawn remembered he had some butane in his pack. "Where'd I leave my backpack?"

"I'm not the keeper of your pack."

"I'll be right back," Shawn said, heading for the house.

"Hurry up. We still need to fetch the liar."

...

The closet was dark and smelled of old lady's perfume. Inside, a young woman, about the age of thirty-five, was awake and contemplating her next move. Her mouth was gagged with an old dirty sock, and it was duct-taped in place around her head and neck. Her feet were tied together, and her hands were tied behind her back. She had not seen the light of day for several hours. Just outside the door, she could hear the sounds of one of her captors rustling around in the hallway.

"Where'd I put that pack?" he said to himself.

The closet door opened up, and a flood of bright light shot into the closet. It was painful to the woman's eyes, so she closed them tightly and pulled herself into the corner as snugly as she could muster. She had been raped several times over by each of her two captors. Her and her husband had been mugged on their trek east by two men.

"Hello, pretty," Shawn said. "I almost forgot about you."

The woman began to squirm because she knew what was next.

Shawn began to wrestle with her.

The woman had a strong will and didn't hesitate to resist her attacker. Even though both of her legs were tied together, she kicked like a mule at the man until he punched her in the mouth. The hit rang her head and she gave up the fight. Shawn pulled her out of the closet by her feet and stood over her. No sooner than he had started to undo his belt, the woman heard a loud *thump* sound and the man fell on top of her. Behind him, another man was standing. A man she had never seen before. She didn't know what to expect; fearing the worst, she pulled herself out from underneath Shawn and began to crawl back into the closet, where she screamed through the dirty sock. Her screams were muffled, but Larry heard them from his position outside.

"Are you on that pretty girl again?" Larry called out to Shawn.

The woman looked up at the new man, and he had his finger up to his mouth, saying, "Shhh. I'm not here to hurt you. I'm going to take that thing out of your mouth, but you have to promise me you're not going to scream."

The woman nodded her head.

"My name's Darrick," he said, taking the gag out of her mouth.

"They'll kill you," she said in a soft voice.

"Not if I get the drop on them," he answered. "How many of them are there?"

AFTER THE PULSE I BOOK 1 I HOMESTEAD

She looked at her rescuer with thankful eyes and answered, "More than you can handle alone."

"There's one out back, one here, and I killed one at my homestead. Are there more than that?" he asked, untying the woman's hands and feet.

"I've only heard rumors, but from what I heard, they're like a plague of locusts. They're just not here. Supposedly, they're somewhere east of here. They keep rambling on about an omen."

"An omen? What sort of omen?"

"I don't know much else," she answered, tired and exhausted.

"What's your name?"

"Kara."

"Kara, I'm going to head around to the south side of the house. Do you think you can distract the man who's outside so I can get the drop on him?"

"Just say when."

...

Larry grew tired of waiting for Shawn to fetch his lighter and butane, so he decided to try to catch them on fire just using a Bic. As he sat there flicking his lighter, he heard a feminine voice from the back door of the house.

"Hey, big boy."

Larry looked up and saw that Kara was free from her bonds. He stood up to walk towards her, but didn't make the distance. A shot rang out through the countryside, and a pink mist blew out from the face of Larry as he fell dead.

Behind him, Darrick was holding his high-caliber rifle. "Not that I'm keeping score, but that's the second man I've killed today."

"Wanna make it three?" she said, hoping he'd finish the job and knock off her attacker, who was still lying unconscious on the hallway floor.

Page **40** of **181**

"You go ahead. I'm looking for my brother, Jimmie Mitchell. Have you seen him? Tall, slim, beard and mustache?"

"Not for weeks."

"Weeks? He turned up missing today."

"Me and my partner met your brother a couple of weeks ago. We were heading east when we found Jimmie's homestead. We didn't chat long, but he mentioned his name and gave us some jarred tomatoes. I only remember because he etched his initials on the top of the jars. J-M, right?"

Darrick nodded, then continued his focus on Kara's story.

"When these guys found us, they shot my partner, JR, and kept me around. They found me more useful. I guess they figured JR would cause them more trouble than he'd be worth. They said they were scouting west, and they took me with them. So I ended up backtracking to this point. I can't tell you the horrors I've had to endure at the hands of these vermin. As heavy a toll as that taxed me; I don't have it in me to kill a man. You go ahead and finish what you started," she concluded.

Darrick went back into the house. Kara heard the gun go off and knew that the task was now complete. She looked up into the heavens with a grateful heart and then closed her eyes. She felt the sun shining on her face as she took the time to enjoy its warm embrace for the first time in quite a while.

Darrick stepped back out onto the porch and asked, "What now?"

"I don't have anywhere to go," she answered.

Darrick felt responsible for her as he considered her answer. "I guess you can come back with me until you decide. It's just me, my wife, my son, my brother and his wife. But, for now, you can help me look for Jimmie," he said, bending down to Larry's body to pull the rifle off his back. He handed it to Kara. "You know how to use this thing?"

"Sure, just point the boom stick at the bad guy, make sure it's on *fire*, and pull the trigger, right?"

"That'll get the job done. There's an old livestock barn on the north side of the property. It's the only place I haven't checked yet."

Darrick walked off toward the old barn, and Kara stayed in the backyard, considering what her next move would be. She looked at the carnage and considered her own future. When she looked into the woods, she saw a blue-colored object that neither she nor Darrick had noticed. Kara walked closer to it and saw a dead man partially covered in woodland debris. She walked towards it and rolled the stiff man over. It was Jimmie Mitchell. The nice man who had given her and her partner a couple of cans of tomatoes. She ran out of the woods and into the front yard of the property, where she met Darrick. Her intentions were one thing, but getting them to work for her was another.

"There's nobody in there," he told her as he came walking up.

"Maybe he's already headed back home?"

"Could be. I guess we won't know until we go find out."

She couldn't reason within herself why she did it, but the lie made Kara feel bad. In truth, she didn't have it in her to tell her rescuer that his brother was dead in the woods. Now she had this nagging secret in her head that was haunting her before she even stepped off the property. It was a problem that she'd have to manage, one way or another.

"I think I'm going to have to turn down your offer to return with you," she said out of the blue.

"Why? Where will you go? Where will you stay?"

"I don't know. I came from the west, and there's trouble to the east. There's colder temperatures to the north. Maybe I should head south?"

"Alone?"

"I can't be bothering you and your family. You've got a missing brother and…" Kara could barely keep the lie inside. She was convincing herself that she wasn't lying, she was only holding the truth from him. A truth that would spare him pain. Whether a lie of commission or a lie of omission, she was still lying to Darrick. He overlooked her behavior. After all, she had been held prisoner for months. Her wrists, ankles, and facial bruising were a testament to her mental and physical toughness. Her spirit was impressively upbeat for a person who had spent so much time in captivity and torture.

She broke down and started crying. Her tears were a mixture of liberation and guilt. It caught Darrick off guard. He moved in to hold her, but she refused him.

Darrick backed away, saying, "Okay, okay, I get it. You don't want to be touched. I'm just –"

Kara interrupted him. She decided to come out with the truth. "It's not that. It's –"

Darrick interrupted Kara. "You don't have to explain anything to me. I don't know what you've been through, and you don't have to relive it."

"Darrick, I –"

"No," he interrupted again. Whatever you have to say can wait until you're ready."

Kara knew what he was thinking, and it had nothing to do with his missing brother, Jimmie.

"And you're coming back with me. You're going to have to learn to trust again. Between Carissa, Tonya, and my son, you'll find somebody to connect with."

"Are you sure your wife will be fine with you bringing a girl home?"

Darrick began leading the way back to the Mitchell homestead. "One as pretty as you, probably not. But she'll come to understand."

Kara began to follow. "Which one is your wife?"

"Tonya is my wife. Carissa is my sister-in-law, and Andy is my son."

"How long have you and Tonya been married?"

"About ten years, give or take. It's hard to tell these days, you know, no calendar and all."

"What's she like?"

"She's headstrong and determined. Not one I'd mess with if I were a girl," Darrick answered, catching on to her interest in him. He couldn't help but feed into her line of questions. She was a pretty woman and intelligent. She had a natural allure that made him give in. "She's sick with ovarian cancer. We don't know exactly how far along it is. Somewhere between stages three and four, we think, based on the information we had before the Pulse. It's hard to say. It's been unchecked for a while now."

"I'm sorry to hear that. How far is it to your homestead?"

"You said you've been there. It's Jimmie's place. Well, it's our place, as in mine and Jimmie's. It's been our family homestead for generations. I can't believe I almost forgot to tell you about our dad."

"Your dad, also? Are you sure there's room for six?"

"Seven," Darrick corrected.

"Huh?"

"There will be seven. Me, Tonya, Carissa, Dad, Andy, you, and Jimmie, when we find him – if he's not home already."

"Oh yeah, Jimmie," she said in a submissive tone. How long was she going to be able to carry on this lie? She had tried to tell Darrick, but he'd shushed her. Not once, but twice. Half of the conviction she was feeling had subsided because he refused to listen to her. The other half of the weight was still a heavy burden that, for the time being, she was willing to bear.

Darrick caught the skip in their conversation. He thought nothing of it. Kara had been through so much, so virtually everything he thought was off about her he contributed to her recent history.

"My brother is the eldest of two. He was still living at home with Mom and Dad when I left for the military. Next thing I know, Mom's dead and Dad has old timer's disease. So I apologize in advance for any weird behaviors you may witness at the Mitchell homestead."

"I doubt anything I witness will be worse than what I've been through."

Darrick almost felt bad for leading her into the point she made. He wanted to apologize, but since she brought it up, he asked the burning question that was nagging at his mind. "Tell me about the men I killed? You mentioned they have a larger group?"

Kara and Darrick continued to trudge along the trail back to his homestead. They had nothing better to do than talk, so she was more than willing to share all she knew, which wasn't much.

"They kept talking about a man named *Denver*. I think I heard them say his nickname was *Gibby*, but I'm not completely sure. They seem pretty fearful of him. They talked about the group being *large and in charge*, but never mentioned the actual size."

"Did they happen to mention what direction they were moving in or what their intentions were?"

"That's the crazy thing – they talked like they're not heading in any particular direction. They're like locusts. They consume everything wherever they are and then move on to the next source."

"Did they happen to mention where they are now?"

"No. Just somewhere east."

Enclave Camp
Several miles east

High above the earth, a murder of crows circled. They formed a dark spirally vortex that descended several yards. For the survivors on the ground, they were nothing new. Everywhere the survivors went, the crows were sure to follow. What started as a pair grew into a murder of several dozen. They circled overhead continuously, following the survivors wherever they roamed. They disappeared in the night sky, and in the morning when the sun pierced through, they appeared once again overhead. What was their purpose, you might ask? The large group of survivors left many dead in their wake. Man's flesh, trash, and debris were all worthy for the crows' food. Human flesh was the most popular. Natural and processed foods were gobbled up by the group. They left little to eat for the crows, aside from corpses.

The evening hours were pushing in, and Denver had a very strict protocol in place. Scouts were sent out in particular teams of two on certain days of the week. They were required to report back one hour prior to sunset in two days' time, without exception. This schedule was made, kept, and enforced by a man named Rueben Reisner, but everybody called him *Ten-Stitches* because of the scar that ran diagonally across his face. Rumor had it, Rueben had been with Denver since the beginning. The stories were that Denver and Rueben escaped from a psych ward when the Pulse happened. The maximum-security hospital shut down, and the employees abandoned their jobs once they learned that there would be no more checks. Nobody ever bothered to investigate the rumors because there was never a need to question the validity that Denver and Rueben were indeed insane. The only thing that mattered to this very large group of survivors was the fact that their bellies had food in them. The way Denver managed them was second to that.

Rueben was standing outside the ranch that had been serving them for months. There had been ample amounts of cattle, hogs, chickens, horses, and smaller animals prior to their arrival months ago. Now, as time would have it, those numbers had dropped. He looked down at his hand. Held tightly in his dirty fingers, a piece of paper was blowing in the wind. He would look up at the two formations of men standing before him and then back down at the paper.

"Has anybody seen Max, Shawn and Larry?"

Rueben was a big man at a staggering six feet seven inches tall and weighing in at 270 pounds. If truth be known, there wasn't a single person standing in those formations that was interested in saying anything that would make him upset.

The men looked at each other. Some of them shrugged their shoulders, and others shook their heads.

One formation of men was fifteen strong. That served as five scouting parties. Six with Max, Shawn and Larry, but they were missing. Rueben was a stickler for timeliness. His schedule worked flawlessly most of the time. Two formations of eighteen men. Thirty-two in all. One group reports in, and the other is sent out. But on this occasion, there was one group of eighteen and another of fifteen. That didn't sit well with the schedule keeper. What if Denver got upset and blamed him? This matter had to be dealt with before he spoke a word of it to Denver.

There were no functioning watches or clocks, so it was custom to use an older more reliable method to tell time. Rueben looked toward the sun with his arm outstretched and his hand making the hand sign for *drink*. With his pinky and thumb outstretched from the horizon to the sun, he figured that they were one hour from sunset. It was unusual for the men to be late. The last time Max, Larry and Shawn didn't show up for roll call, they had been flogged with a horse's whip thirty times each. This time meant certain death. Denver didn't tolerate insubordination. If the men didn't do exactly as they were told, then severe penalties followed. The first offense was torture. The second offense was execution. Denver believed everybody deserved a second chance, but there was no such thing as three strikes and you're out. Rueben knew this.

He let out a grunt and said, "Group A, fall out and get some rest. Be back here in two days' time, one hour before sunset. Group B, stand fast."

Max, Shawn and Larry's group scattered from formation, afraid of what was about to happen. Rueben walked up and down the line of scouts who were about to be sent out. The way he figured it, there were fifteen in one group and eighteen in the other. Those were numbers that couldn't be reconciled without making an adjustment.

Rueben had a pistol that he carried on his side. Nobody had the courage to challenge Rueben. When his pistol was pulled, everybody was quiet. They knew there was going to be blood, so they watched and waited. The pistol was back in its holster after the three men hit the ground. They weren't head shots, but they were fatal abdominal shots. In earlier times, before the Pulse, they might have survived, but since it was Rueben who shot them, they were to be left for dead.

"The rest of you can group yourselves in teams of three and head out. Be back here in two days' time, one hour before sunset. Go find Max, Larry, and Shawn. Double rations for the man who finds them. Triple for the man who finds them alive."

The men scattered, knowing full well that they had a mission to find those missing men.

Standing off to the side of Rueben was a man by the name of Cornelius Woods. He was the group's spiritual advisor. Everybody called him "the Rev," but he insisted they just call him Cornelius.

Rueben didn't like the Rev. He had been jealous of him since the first day he arrived. Denver was a spiritual man, albeit he suffered from paranoid schizophrenia. There wasn't a soul in the group who knew Denver's mind but Denver. The thing that made Rueben so jealous of the Rev was that, some of the time, when Denver would become upset and frustrated, he would call on the Rev; for Rueben that gave the Rev access into Denver's mind that he didn't have. Rueben's mental diagnosis had never been determined prior to his commitment. He had been classified as Unfit to Stand Trial and sent into the mental health system, where he later met Denver.

With a sneer in his voice, he looked over at the Rev and said, "What are you looking at?"

The Rev responded by walking away.

Paranoia began to escalate in Rueben's mind.

What if he tells Denver that three men never returned from scouting? That would make me look weak.

Rueben followed the Rev around the corner of the ranch house.

"Hey," he growled.

The Rev stopped and turned around.

Rueben just wanted to warn him in his own way. "How many times have I told you not to be snaking around me?"

"Snaking?"

"You know I don't like it when you're watching over my shoulder."

"I was just passing through. I enjoy the evening breeze."

Rueben wasn't buying his story. Whether from paranoia or a nose for deception. "Just find your ruck. It's almost curfew."

The Rev walked off toward the pole barn. It used to be full of cattle, but they were all wrangled up and herded to the pasture so that the group could have some shelter. His spot was in the corner over against the door, where he could be called on and answer to Denver in a hurry if he had to. He plopped down on the floor and leaned back against the wall.

"I've never seen you here before," the man next to him said. The Rev was oblivious to the number of people who were gathering in the barn. The last few days he had been dealing with several issues of his own. He was aware of the fact that he was going through psychological stages that were affecting his judgment and attitude. That was why he didn't answer the stranger to his left.

"My name's Byron," the stranger tried again.

"Cornelius," the Rev answered. "My name's Cornelius."

"How long you been here, Cornelius?"

"A few weeks now. I think. I really don't know anymore."

"Do you have family?"

Cornelius was already slightly annoyed at the questions the man was asking. The last question, in particular, solicited an emotional response. Cornelius covered his face with his hands and pulled his knees up to support his elbows as he wept.

Byron had struck a nerve. He looked to his left and saw his wife and two daughters sitting there by his side. He knew that Cornelius had lost his loved ones, and he felt horrible for snooping. He didn't know what to say, so he said the first thing that came to his mind.

"When the Enclave first came through my area, I thought about resisting them. I knew that if I did, my decision to do so would cost me my life and probably their lives, too. I don't know what you've lost, but if you want to talk, I'm here to listen."

Cornelius was used to doing the listening. Byron was offering him something greater than he could repay: an ear. He sniffed his runny nose and wiped his eyes on his shoulder. His hands were no longer covering his face when he turned his face upward with his head leaning against the wall of the barn. There was a secret he wanted to tell Byron, but he knew he couldn't trust him enough to say it. So he kept that to himself and began to share what he could.

"I used to live in a little community east of here. It was me and my wife; she was four months pregnant when the Pulse happened. I was at work, like many Americans, and panicked. I spent so much time trying to find out what was going on that I neglected my greatest priority –"

"Your wife?"

Cornelius nodded his head. "If I had left for home sooner –"

"It's okay. If you can't talk, that's fine."

Cornelius let out a large exhale. "I'm sorry."

"There's no reason to be sorry, Cornelius."

"I worked an hour from home," he added with a look at Byron. "An hour by car. It took me a day to get to her. When I did, she wasn't there. I waited so long. The community banded together and tried to make something of what was left. The politicians were a bunch of left-wing idealists, so the first time a man was shot for stealing, they confiscated our firearms. Ten more people died during that squabble. About a year and a half after that, rumors of an omen began to circulate. Nobody believed the stories – a mass of migrating crows and boogeymen that lived in their shadows."

"I heard those stories, too, more recently though. I remember seeing the crows for days on end. Curiosity got me. That's when we were captured."

Cornelius looked at Byron and wondered why he hadn't noticed that there were no kids and very few wives. He wanted to say something, but fear of what might come gripped his heart thinking about it. Cornelius felt that he might be worth something to Denver now, but anything could change. He wasn't about to do something stupid that might tip the balance.

"How were you captured?" Byron asked when he saw Cornelius was struggling with his emotions again.

"I remember attending a town hall meeting with the mayor and other leaders of the community about the rumors of the Omen. We didn't know the group as the Enclave at that point; all we knew were that those birds kept getting closer and closer until the shooting started. It didn't last long. There were only a few armed men. The rest of us ran and hid. I went to the church and hid in the pulpit." Cornelius realized he'd already said too much. His secret was out, so he finished his story. "That's when they found me. They said Denver had killed his last preacher and they needed a new one. I've been playing the part ever since."

Byron realized his storyteller was exposing himself to danger for even speaking the words openly. He looked about to see that no one was eavesdropping. The coast was clear.

"Your secret's safe with me, preacher man."

Cornelius looked up at Byron again. "Byron?"

"Yeah?"

He wanted to warn him about his family's safety, but he was afraid for his own. "Have a good night," he said, supplanting his original thought.

"Good night, preacher."

Cornelius rolled over and closed his eyes. Byron could tell he was dealing with more than he was letting on. He assumed Cornelius was dealing with Stockholm syndrome. He was right. Cornelius was staying loyal to Denver out of fear.

It wasn't yet dark, but Cornelius's eyes were closed, and his mind was adrift with the knowledge that Byron's family probably wouldn't survive the Cleanse.

Mitchell Homestead

Tonya and Carissa sat on the living room couch and watched Andy play with Jimmie's childhood toys in the quickly dimming front room. Carissa had barely said a word since Darrick had stepped off to look for her husband. The silence was awkward and made Andy's playtime seem almost deafening. Hoping to break the ice, Tonya asked Carissa a question. "So how did you and Jimmie meet?"

Carissa stood up and walked over to the window. For a second, Tonya thought she was ignoring her. Instead, she peeled the curtain back and said, "You see that car over there in the corner of the yard?"

Tonya stood up and walked to the window. "Yeah?"

"That's a 1974 Torino. It belonged to my daddy's daddy." Carissa's mind was now on her dad, and Tonya could tell her distraction was working. "Would you believe that I was driving down that road when it ran out of gas right in front of this house?"

"No kidding? How'd it run after the Pulse?"

"I don't know. Jimmie said that some of the older cars that were made before computer chips could withstand an EMP. I think it has something to do with a lack of sensitive electrical systems. Basically, there's not too much in it that an EMP can damage."

"So why aren't you driving it around now?"

"And risk getting carjacked? No, thank you! I'll let the weeds grow up around it. It's empty anyway. We haven't had gasoline around here in some time. Jimmie worries that if we overreach for resources that we absolutely don't need, we can become dependent upon it and risk detection."

"Jimmie sounds like a nervous Nelly."

"Maybe, but he's kept us alive this long. I needed someone like him in my life. Not just to keep me safe, but to make me feel safe. I lost that when my daddy died."

"I'm sorry. When did he pass?"

"The Pulse killed him. He was sick anyway. He had the cancer and he was on a vent. Could barely breathe on his own. The health care system failed him. I was there when it happened."

Tonya watched as Carissa's eyes welled with tears. She'd taken her from one stressor to another. She felt like she couldn't win for trying.

"He suffocated to death. He was squeezing my hand and –"

Carissa started to choke up. Tonya moved in closer and pulled her in for a hug. "I'm sorry you had to endure that."

Carissa sobbed on Tonya's shoulder. "If something has happened to Jimmie…"

"Nothing's happened to Jimmie. You just get that out of your head. Darrick went out to find him. If there's one thing Darrick does good, it's find people."

"How do you get good at finding people?" Carissa asked, pulling away from Tonya's hug and wiping her nose.

"He doesn't talk about it too much. He won't admit it, but I think he has some issues that he brought back from the war. He called it a QRF."

"What's that?"

"I don't have a clue. It had something to do with getting in fast and getting out fast. Like I said, he doesn't talk much about it."

"I hope you're right. I hope he can find Jimmie."

"You have my word. My Darrick will find Jimmie."

There was a knock at the back.

Carissa and Tonya stood motionless and looked at each other. "I didn't hear it. Was that the secret knock?" Carissa asked. They'd securely fastened the house when they came back in.

"Open up. It's me," they heard Darrick say.

Both of the women ran excitedly to the back door. They reached it at the same time and laughed as their hands fumbled over the deadbolt. Laughter turned into silence when the door was open.

"Where's Jimmie?" Carissa asked.

"I thought he came back," Darrick answered. "He's not at the Berts'."

"No, he didn't come back," Carissa said, her voiced raised. She looked at Tonya. "He's good at finding people, huh?"

Tonya felt bad. She had so much trust in Darrick's capabilities and was surprised when he didn't come back with his brother. She was left speechless.

Carissa stood there for a moment, pondering her next move. Obviously frustrated at both Darrick and Tonya for getting her hopes up, she said, "Fine, I'll go find him myself," charging past Darrick and Kara.

Tonya saw Darrick's company. "Who's the chick?"

Darrick ignored Tonya's question, choosing to focus on Carissa's rash move toward the Berts' homestead. "Where do you think you're going?" he called out to her. She was well on her way. Darrick ran after her, grabbing her by the arm and pulling her around.

"I'm going to do what you couldn't," she shot back.

"It's not safe out there. You'll be killed."

"If I die, it'll be trying to find my husband!"

Kara was listening to the argument. Tonya was looking at Kara. She was studying her and couldn't help but recognize her bruises. She wasn't so much concerned about them as she was what she felt might be her competition. Darrick had never given his wife a reason to doubt his fidelity, but the stranger was an attractive woman.

Kara's attention was turned to the argument between Darrick and Carissa. Muffled sounds were all that Tonya was hearing when Kara suddenly blurted out, "I know where Jimmie is."

Darrick and Carissa were so heated that they didn't hear the comment. Tonya heard the first time.

Kara raised her voice over the dispute. "I know where Jimmie is," she repeated.

Darrick stood still and in a state of confusion as Carissa left her brother-in-law to confront the stranger.

"Do I know you from somewhere?" Carissa asked.

"My partner and I passed through here a couple of weeks ago. Your Jimmie gave us some food. I know where he's at."

Darrick heard the comment. "What do you mean you know where he's at? Why did you follow me all the way home if –" Darrick immediately assumed the worst-case scenario. He grabbed the woman and overpowered her to the ground.

"What are you doing?" Carissa shouted. "She knows where Jimmie is."

"She doesn't know where Jimmie is. She just wanted to see where the homestead is, and now she wants to lead us away. Think about it."

Darrick was struggling with Kara when she said, "You're the one who invited me here. I don't want anything from you."

Darrick looked up at Tonya, who was still standing near the kitchen door. "Fetch me some rope."

Tonya ran into the house.

"Let me go," Kara cried out. Her mind began to flash back to her recent past. Memories of rape and segregation darkened her mind. Through the darkness she heard Carissa's voice. "Darrick, she said she knows where Jimmie is."

"She's lying, Carissa!"

"I can show you," Kara pleaded.

"You can tell me," Darrick said.

Kara became nervously quiet.

"What if she's telling the truth, Darrick?"

"It's too much of a risk."

"Carissa, right?" Kara asked.

"Yeah?"

"I know where Jimmie is, but –"

"But what?"

"I'm telling you this now because it's too dangerous to go back."

Tonya came running out of the house with some rope and handed it to Darrick. She was all too happy to see that Darrick wasn't enthralled with the woman's good looks. Darrick began tying the woman's wrists behind her back.

"Please don't," she cried.

Carissa, taken aback by her words of knowledge of Jimmie's whereabouts and her cries, lunged toward Darrick and knocked him over. Kara stood up and went to work shaking off the rope that hadn't been knotted yet. Carissa jumped between Kara and Darrick while he was standing back up. He was content seeing that Kara wasn't running away. That bought him some time to confront them both.

"If she's lying, we could all be in serious jeopardy," he said, arm raised and finger pointing.

Elder Mitchell came barging out the back door. "What's all the ruckus?"

The old man stopped dead in his tracks when he saw Kara. "Tina?"

Darrick rolled his eyes and dropped his arm. Tina was Darrick and Jimmie's mother. She had been deceased for some time. "Not now, Dad," Darrick said.

Kara knew by Darrick's earlier description that the old man had Alzheimer's disease.

Darrick passed in front of Carissa to assist with his father. When he did, Kara left her safety behind Carissa and ran up next to him and whispered, "The woods."

Darrick didn't catch her drift. "The woods? What are you talking about?"

Kara was too nervous to clarify any further. It was obvious she was keeping a secret, a secret that became suddenly clear to Darrick as he thought about her two-word clue.

"Oh God," he said, realizing what she meant. It was the cue words and the sad look in her teary eyes that gave it away. Kara knew Darrick was a good man. She had no ill-intended plot, as Darrick had wrongfully suspected. She was just a woman too afraid to tell the truth for fear of causing pain to people she barely knew.

Carissa was confused. She heard Darrick question the stranger's whisper, but didn't manage to put it together the way Darrick had. Perhaps out of a lack of intuition, or maybe a lack of willingness to accept another tragedy into her life. "What's going on?" Carissa asked, her eyes now filling with tears.

Darrick studied the horizon, pacing back and forth with an intense fervor to take action. The sun was almost down, and it was too late to leave. He looked at Carissa, knowing each of them was going to have a long night.

Carissa looked at the stranger. "What did you whisper to him?"

Kara looked at Darrick, but all he said was, "We'll bring Jimmie home in the morning."

Carissa now understood the gravity of the stranger's whisper. Her knees buckled beneath her and she fell to the ground. Darrick reached down and pulled her up for an embrace.

Tonya felt lost in the moment and took elder Mitchell by the hand and led him back into the house. She looked back over her shoulder to see that Kara was staying by Darrick's side. Tonya wanted to, but something about the situation drove her away. She didn't care to speak out or to share any feelings or thoughts that might have been on her mind. She just wanted to be somewhere else. A hint of jealousy was upon her. Watching her man caress another woman, even a woman in mourning, was affecting her judgment. It never had before. Why now? Maybe it was because of Kara. Or maybe it was because she was tired and feeling emotional. Whatever the reason, Tonya put old man Mitchell to bed. The whole time he was calling for his deceased wife, Tina, the woman Tonya knew to be Kara, the woman by Darrick's side.

"Where is she?" elder Mitchell asked.

"She's outside. Try to get some sleep."

"Why's she outside? I took care of the tractor thingy. She thinks she can fix it, but I've had my hands on that ol' John Deere for years," he said, holding them up. He was shocked to see how old looking his hands were. "What happened to my hands?"

"You're getting old," she answered. "Your hands aren't what they used to be."

"Old? I'll show you old," he said, trying to sit up. Tonya was able to hold him on the bed with just one hand. Elder Mitchell was shocked at his lack of strength. He was deeply confused, not knowing that he was a sick man. He relaxed backwards, and his mind roamed for a second. He spoke two words that made Tonya believe he was having a moment of clarity.

"Where's Jimmie?"

"Jimmie's –" Tonya hesitated, not knowing what answer she might give. "Jimmie's with Tina," she answered thoughtfully.

"Good. I love that boy. I can't believe he's twelve years old already. I have to be strict on him because if I don't, the world'll chew him up and spit him out. I see it getting more dangerous all the time, and I worry about that."

Tonya considered his words and finished tucking him in. "I know you love your wife and son. They'll be in as soon as they get done trying to show you up with their handiwork on the tractor."

Elder Mitchell looked upon the face of the pretty lady. The room was dark, and he tried to recognize her, but he couldn't. "Who are you again?"

"I'm a nobody. Good night, James," she said, kissing him on the forehead before leaving.

The next morning
August 14th
Darrick awakened with the mindset to go find Jimmie. It had been a long sleepless night. He had lain awake much of the night,

staring into the darkness, contemplating the recovery of his brother's body. It was also a sad night. No sooner than he gained control of his tears, he would think about Jimmie and would whisk away to their childhood, releasing a deluge of tears. The sniffles that followed kept Tonya up much of the night. She knew Darrick was mourning the loss of his brother, so she did little to interfere in the grieving process.

Darrick might have been sorrowful over the death of Jimmie, but one thing angered him above all: the manner in which he had been discarded, like human refuse. He was glad he'd killed those three men; however, in the back of his mind he knew a reckoning was to follow. Those men belonged to a group known only as the Omen, and he knew nothing about them. Darrick knew that he would have to keep his wits about him if he was to keep his family and homestead safe from discovery.

Before Darrick could leave, he first needed to confront Kara as to why she hadn't told him his brother was dead. He needed some answers to the questions that made his mind roam all night long. Kara, Andy, Darrick, and Tonya all slept in the front room. Darrick took the chair and slept upright with a rifle in his lap. Kara and Tonya slept on the couch with their heads on opposing ends. Andy had a pallet on the floor.

"Hey, wake up," Darrick said, nudging Kara awake with his foot. His actions not only woke up Kara, but also caught the attention of his wife, Tonya.

"What are you doing, Darrick?" Tonya asked him.

"I want some answers."

Kara collected herself and sat up on the couch. She looked at Darrick and rubbed the sleep from her eyes.

He bent over to pick the backpack up off the floor and slung it over one shoulder. He already had a rifle slung over the other shoulder and pistol on his side. "Tell me. Carissa's upstairs asleep. I understand why you whispered to me last night about Jimmie, but what I don't understand is why you didn't tell me. We were right there, and you said nothing."

"I tried to tell you. You shushed me, like, three times."

Darrick knew she was right. "You should have led with a different word or something. I don't know, but that was important, and you shouldn't have let me leave without my brother."

"I'm sorry," she said, standing up. "My mind has been a little preoccupied with the things I've been through, so forgive me if I seem a little selfish."

Darrick only had a notion of what she had been through. He felt bad for expecting so much of her. His mind was racing with many issues, but the mass of them would have to be managed later. Right now, he needed to grab some breakfast and get his mind right for the trip to the Berts' homestead. "Whatever," he conceded. "I'm going back to the Berts'."

The wood floor creaked just around the corner. Darrick, Tonya, and Kara looked toward the edge of the hallway. It was Carissa. She had listened to most of the conversation and revealed herself when Darrick said his last word.

She was looking squarely at Kara. "How long have you known about my Jimmie?"

"Since yesterday. Right before Darrick talked me into following him home."

"Wait! What?" Tonya interjected. Looking at Darrick, she asked him, "You talked her into following you home?"

"Tonya, not now!" he said, hoping to avoid a conflict with his wife.

She huffed and shook her head, but she wasn't ready to throw in the towel.

"Why didn't you tell Darrick yesterday?" Carissa asked, as if Tonya's argument was insignificant.

"Didn't you hear what she said?" Darrick defended. "She tried to tell me three times, but I wouldn't have it. She was tortured and –"

Darrick cut himself off, realizing he was about to mention something that might trigger Kara. He thought a moment, then corrected himself. "– and abused."

"We're literally in the apocalypse, Darrick. How can anyone use an excuse?"

"I don't have time for this, ladies. I'm going after Jimmie."

"I'm coming with you," Carissa said.

"No, you're not," Darrick argued. "You need to stay here and help Tonya take care of Dad . She can't handle him alone."

Carissa knew Darrick was right. "Fine, but you'd better not disappoint," she added.

Darrick was done arguing. He looked through his assault pack to make sure he had everything he needed. Jimmie had a few things lying around the house that Darrick had put together in an assault pack. There was a camouflaged burlap blind that duck hunters would use to conceal their position, a few loose rounds for the hunting rifle he was carrying, a buck knife, binoculars, some 550 paracord (about fifty feet's worth), and a flare gun with two flares.

"I'm coming along, then," Kara said.

"You've been through enough," Darrick said. "Besides, not too sure I can trust you anymore."

"Because I protected you?"

"Because you lied to me."

"Not telling isn't lying."

"Close enough."

"Doesn't change things."

"What do you mean?"

"I'm still coming."

"No, you're not."

"Watch me."

Darrick was frustrated and tired of arguing. "Fine. If you get in a jam, you're on your own."

"Wouldn't be the first time."

Kara grabbed one of the packs that was lying on the floor and threw it over her shoulder. Tonya jumped up from her position and snatched the backpack from Kara's shoulder.

"That's my pack and you're not taking it."

Darrick was done with all of it. He let out a loud sigh and headed out the back door. Kara followed closely behind.

Tonya and Carissa were left standing in the front room area. Carissa look at Tonya. Tonya shrugged her shoulders and headed to the bedroom.

Just outside, Kara was chasing Darrick toward the Berts' homestead. Her legs were quite a bit shorter than Darrick's, so she was moving twice as fast.

"Wait up," she called out.

"Keep up or stay back," he said.

"Look, I'm sorry I didn't say anything."

"You tried to, right? You tried to, and I didn't want to hear what you wanted to say. Sad thing is that you wanted to tell me and I shut you out."

"So are we good or what?"

Darrick stopped in his tracks and turned around to face her. "I want us to be, Kara, but this isn't a lost puppy or something that was borrowed and was lost. This is my brother. You left him lying in the woods and hid it from all of us. Even if I wouldn't hear you, you let Carissa think he was still out there. How do you defend against that?"

Kara raised and lowered her arms in frustration. It was a shrug of sorts.

Darrick turned back toward the Berts' and picked up his pace. "I have no idea how you're going to be able to make this up to her," he said. "Me, maybe so, but Carissa? Oh, and let's not forget my wife doesn't seem particularly fond of the idea of my bringing in a woman."

"Okay, that is not on me. You said she'd understand."

"That was before this. I'm bringing my brother home today, and he's been lying in the woods for God knows how long. We're trekking into a potentially dangerous area with six bullets in my pistol and a few loose rounds for the rifle." Darrick stopped again to study Kara. "And you're not even armed," he said, pulling the pistol out of his holster. "Don't worry; it's ready to fire. All you have to do is point the boom stick at the bad guy and pull the trigger." He handed it to Kara.

"Does this mean you trust me now? You were trying to hog-tie me last night."

Darrick ignored the question, choosing instead to turn back toward the Berts' homestead and start walking again.

"You were in the Marines, weren't you?" she asked, trying desperately to get him to open up to her.

"I was."

"What did you do?"

"It doesn't matter."

"You went through a lot, didn't you?"

"Don't worry about it."

"You just seem like a person who's hiding something."

Darrick stopped again and turned around in a fury. "What do you know about –"

His angry gaze met Kara's. She felt like he was burning a hole in her soul. She watched his eyes and waited. They quickly subdued and surrendered to hers.

"It's okay," she said. "You can talk about it with me, and I'll never speak of it again."

She maintained her eye contact. She could almost see his walls coming down.

He turned and started walking again. Just when Kara thought he was about to shut down again, he started talking.

"It started when I was a boy. My dad would send me out back to pick a switch for him to swat me with. I had to come back with the biggest one I could find. If it was too small, he would make me get a clothes hanger out of the closet. I'm not talking about the plastic ones, either. Don't get me wrong, those hurt too, but the metal ones would wrap around and cover more area. In turn, I would go to school and release my aggression on other kids in the school yard. I would get in trouble, get more beatings, and perpetuate the violence. Jimmie was always smarter than me. He caught on and adjusted. He still got it, but not as much as I did. If he interfered with the beatings that I was receiving, he would get his and mine. That's all it was in the end. Jimmie started taking them for me every time. Up until the time I left. I ran away at sixteen and took care of myself until I was eighteen. I left Jimmie alone with that man and I joined the Marines. I figured it was a good way for me to release some serious aggression issues."

"What happened to you in the Marines?"

"Three years into my service I joined MAGTF."

"Magtaf?"

"It's kind of like a crisis response team."

"How'd that go?"

Darrick didn't answer. She could sense that he was starting to shut down. Whatever vein she had opened up was the issue that was causing him so much pain. It was working him over more so than his childhood trauma.

Darrick broke his silence by asking Kara a question. "What did you do before the Pulse?"

Darrick couldn't see it, but Kara was smiling. "I was a clinical psychologist."

Darrick stopped and caught her smiling at him. "Have you been shrinking my head this whole time?"

"Hey, you didn't ask, so I didn't tell."

"So, are you gonna be able to cure my issues, doc?"

"No, but I can help you get through them. That's about the extent of knowledge. If it were two or three years ago, I'd refer you to a psychiatrist for some Valium or something."

"So I need meds?"

"Only for your anxiety issues. But that's neither here nor there. What we can start working on is getting you to open up so that you don't have to bear the weight alone."

"We need to keep moving. It's not smart to stand still," he said.

Kara knew he was still shutting her out. She wasn't going to push him any further today.

Sometime later

Darrick and Kara took up positions behind the rabbit cages of the Berts' homestead.

"We can't be too careful," Darrick said. "We have to assume that somebody's here until we clear the house and we know for sure."

"Why can't we just run over to the wood line, grab your brother, and beat the dirt?"

"If you remember right, there's a door on the back side of that house, along with a few windows. If anybody's in there, they'll have the advantage over us."

"Good point."

"You keep to head-shrinking and leave the security to me."

Kara smirked at him.

"Here's what I need you to do," he said. "Stay here and cover this door. If I come running out, be ready to shoot whoever comes out after me. Got it?"

"Got it."

Darrick slowly stood into a crouched position. His military training taught him that he needed to maintain a low profile while moving. Smaller profiles meant smaller targets. He had no intention of becoming some killer's target. He moved into position against the house and listened for anything out of the ordinary. Nothing. It was a dead calm. The birds whistled in the background, and the morning breeze blew through the trees, causing the leaves to rustle.

Now for the dangerous part.

Darrick poked his head up and peered in through the window. The shades were closed, but he could see in through the sides.

No movement. Time to open the door.

Darrick had a flashback.

QRF Typhoon Base
1st Battalion 2nd Marines Headquarters
Musayib, Iraq
Babil Province – 10 years earlier

"Okay, listen up, Marines," Captain Horowitz shouted. "I know you guys are a reaction force, but this one came down from on high. We've received word of a high-value target just south of here right smack in the middle of Musayib."

Captain Horowitz walked around a table that was blocking his reach and pointed to a position on the Euphrates River. "The objective is right here in this building. As you can see, there's no easy access point and it's completely surrounded by Iraqi rubbernecks. Unfortunately, because of the way the things are put together, the inner cordon will be exposed from the east, and there will not be an outer cordon to provide assistance from the west, because the river is outright blocking the approach. The walls that surround the residence are four feet tall, making the breach easy, but we'll need to maintain a low profile to avoid detection. If you're a Devil Dog on the shorter end, then you may need assistance getting over. Sergeants, make sure your small Marines are over the wall first. Don't leave them hanging out to dry.

"I want the TOW thermals to stay river side so you don't have to worry about your backsides being exposed. Battalion has pledged to keep us covered from the west side of the Euphrates.

"Sorens, I want your platoon to provide perimeter security for Rednaur's hard-chargers. Once they breach, there may be light resistance. Dilshad Al Halsheem is the HVT and will have a small security team of five or six of Saddam Hussein's ex-Republican Guard fighters with him; they won't go down without a fight, so make sure you have concussions, smoke, and NVGs to make a hasty snatch 'n grab.

"Any questions?" The captain looked around and saw one hand. "Yes, Corporal?"

"Isn't there something we can drop on that area instead of risking our necks, sir?"

"You're a Marine, Mitchell," the captain read from Darrick's name tape. "Your orders are to make the breach, grab the HVT, and get out. I'll indulge your question just this once. The quarters are tight for this extraction, Devil Dogs. The idea to drop a precision strike was considered, but the powers that be thought it was too risky. The ROEs are loose, but the chance that we injure or kill civies, even on a precision strike, is too great. Besides, it was discussed that if we can take this man alive, we can obtain valuable information that will lead us to the apprehension of Azad el-Amin. As you know, that's a man who's managed to stay two moves ahead of us for the past three weeks."

Captain Horowitz looked around one last time and said, "Dismissed."

Darrick stood up with the rest of his platoon and started making his way back to his barracks.

"Did you have to put me on the spot like that?" Corporal Guy asked.

Mitchell laughed. "You know me. Always looking to add a little spice."

"Can't ever leave good enough alone, can you?"

"Now where's the fun in that?"

Guy laughed.

"You guys can lollygag later," Staff Sergeant Singleton said to them. "Head back to the barracks. Formation's at thirteen hundred hours."

"Aye, Staff Sergeant," Mitchell answered.

"He's had a stick up his butt for the last couple of weeks," Guy said as they were walking back to their Humvee.

"I know. He's getting grouchy in his older years."

"God, I hope I don't get like that when I'm thirty."

"I'll be like that in seven years," Mitchell said.

"You're the saltiest corporal I've ever had the misfortune of working with."

Mitchell knew Guy was joking around. Guy always bantered with him about being busted down from sergeant to corporal for starting fights in E Clubs. Mitchell had made corporal rank at four years. At five years, he made sergeant and got into his first fight with a corpsman at Camp Hansen in Okinawa. After a run-in with some nonjudicial punishment, he was demoted to corporal.

"You gonna re-up again next year?" Guy asked.

"No, man, I think I'm done. I had some stuff in me I needed to get out. I thought fighting would help, but I think I just compounded the problem."

"There's always rehab," Guy joked as they entered their Humvee. "I've got one week before I get out. This'll be my last mission, man. I'm stoked to be going home." Guy could see that Mitchell was thinking about that crush he had back home. He always smiled when he thought of her. "You've got feelings for that girl back in Pleasant Bray, Georgia, don't ya?"

"Tonya? No, man. She was a high school infatuation."

"I heard you talking about her with Wade, not to mention every time I talk about home, you start grinning ear to ear. I know it's not because you miss your pops."

"Busted." Mitchell laughed. "Yeah, I guess I do think about her a lot."

"I guess that explains why you have to get out, eh? Strike while the iron's hot?"

"She's single, Guy. I've been keeping in touch with her."

"Saving 'er letters, too, aren't ya?"

"Yeah. It keeps me sane in this Godforsaken country."

"It is Godforsaken. It's Muslim, man. These hajis'll kill a woman for looking cross-eyed at a man. When you do catch a glimpse of a woman's eyes, it's like, *wow, a woman!* But the men here, they're not even civilized. They're like animals."

"That's why I don't hesitate to pop one every chance I get."

"How many have ya killed?"

"Not sure anymore. A dozen, maybe. I don't know. It's not like I'm keeping score or have somebody to confirm each kill." Mitchell had a couple of seconds of reflection before asking Guy an important question.

"Hey, man?"

"Yeah?"

"I want ya to promise me something."

Guy looked at Mitchell and smirked. "That depends. I don't write blank checks."

"I have a bad feeling about this raid. I want you to promise me that if something happens to me, you'll find my girl, Tonya Ross, back in Lower Georgia, and tell her I had every intention of asking her to marry me."

"Sure, man. We'll be fine. I've done this a time or two. We'll be fine," he reassured him again.

"I know we've got a few raids under our belts, but something just feels different this time. I can't shake it."

Later that night

The mission was supposed to be a surprise raid, but all the clues suggested otherwise. The neighborhood was eerily quiet, and it was hard to silence the gentle rumbles of a platoon of Humvees. The outer cordon (the security element) had tightly sealed off a large area around the target's residence, all except the area against the Euphrates. Guy's unit was the inner cordon (the support element). Their job was to make sure the breaching teams were extracted safely and to provide assistance should things go awry during the raid.

"I don't like this," Mitchell said in a soft voice. He could barely be heard by the driver, who was sitting not two feet away. Mitchell was wearing night-vision goggles and saw several Iraqi men of fighting age standing on the rooftops with cell phones in hand. Some of them were making phone calls.

Corporal Guy was in the turret behind a .50-caliber machine gun. He also had NVGs on and was concerned the same way Mitchell was. Not knowing if Mitchell was seeing what he was seeing, he slouched down out of position of the turret and said, "Mitchell, you be careful out there. This don't smell right."

Mitchell nodded and went back to watching the suspicious red-flag behavior. He picked up the mic and held it up to his mouth. He was about to say something about lookouts when a notification came over the radio:

"Echo Six Tango, Echo Five Sierra, do you see the lookouts? Over."

"Affirmative. Mission is still a go. Over."

Mitchell put the mic back on the radio clip, frustrated that the raid was still on. The Humvee came to a stop, signaling that the inner cordon was in place and it was time for him to exit on foot and rally on the extraction team for a final headcount before making the breach.

"Hey," he heard Guy call out.

Mitchell turned to look up at the gunner.

"You be careful in there. This smells bad," Guy whispered.

Mitchell waved to Guy. The weight of the NVGs prevented him from making any sudden head movements without throwing the fit of the goggles off.

A few moments later, Mitchell was lined up against a wall with the few Marines involved in the extraction. Each of them was mentally preparing themselves for the imminent fight with Halsheem's security team.

Time seemed to slow as they waited for the team leader's signal to move in. When the signal finally came, the first Marine mounted the wall and shot over like it was nothing. Then the second, the third, the fourth, and so on, until it was Mitchell's turn. He was the seventh Marine of eight, so the pressure was a little less than the guys up front, but the threat was real. Mitchell jumped over the wall and looked back to secure the last Marine to go over.

The group reassembled against the house and prepared to breach the door. He couldn't see the team leader, but knew he was placing a charge that would destroy the door's locking system so they could force it open and enter the house. Their left side was against the house, with their right side exposed to the rooftops of neighboring buildings. Mitchell could feel his heart pounding in his chest. This was only his third raid, so he wasn't bringing a whole lot of experience to the table, but it was enough for this particular snatch and grab. The night-vision goggles were cumbersome, but provided him with the visibility he needed. Mitchell looked up and to the right one last time before the detonation went off. On the rooftop of the house next door, he saw a man standing with a cell phone in hand.

This ain't right. Something's wrong, he thought.

There was a loud *boom* and the team began their entry. Mitchell took his eyes off the man on the rooftop and followed his brothers-in-arms into the Halsheem residence. His senses were heightened and his paranoia for something being out of place was haunting him. Gunshots could be heard as he rushed into the house and brought his rifle up into the high ready position.

Something's wrong, he thought again. The gunshots were AK-47s, and he wasn't hearing any return fire. No sooner than the enemy's rifles had started shooting, there were loud explosions heard in the not-so-distant background. They were accompanied by the distinctive sounds of the .50-caliber machine guns. Michell's fears were being realized. It was an ambush. One of the Marines that were ahead of him shouted, "We're in a kill box!" In that moment, the Marines' mission had instantly changed from a raid to survival.

Mitchell could hear the Marines ahead of him starting to return fire. He was patiently waiting for the command to fall back or retreat, and deep inside he knew it wouldn't come. Mitchell was in his seventh year of service and he had never heard the words *retreat* or *fall back* in a combat engagement. He knew the reason his unit was so successful in mission accomplishment was because of their tenacity. Mitchell assumed the radioman was calling for help, so it was a matter of time before the inner cordon sent men into the raid point to provide some assistance. He was wrong.

Outside, a few yards away, the inner cordon was also being fired upon. The Weapons Company Humvees were under heavy AK-47, RPG, and mortar fire attack. The mortar rounds were not precise and were landing rather sloppily around or near the American war machines, causing nothing but havoc and disarray. The RPGs and AK-47s were destroying the security element.

Back in Halsheem's home, Mitchell had made his way through the point of entry. He could now hear a balanced mixture of M4 and AK-47 rifles. When he turned the corner of the next room, he saw two Marines lying on the floor bleeding out, one from the chest and the other from the neck. An Iraqi man shot up out of a hatch in the floor, catching Mitchell off guard with a shot to the abdomen. He returned fire and shot the man in the chest. He was pulled back down into the hatch.

A loud explosion rocked the residence. The percussion shook Mitchell and the team violently. Much of the shooting that had been heard in the eastern room was silenced. The Marines collected themselves, but not before a group of armed insurgents ran into the residence and started shooting.

Mitchell backed up against the wall. Realizing that their formation had been broken and there would be no hope of extraction any time soon, he raised his rifle in the direction of insurgents and started shooting them. They were also shooting, albeit without precision.

Another explosion rocked the house, but this time it came from behind him. The wall exploded inward, knocking him down onto his face. His ears were ringing and his head was numb. He tried to find his bearings. Remembering that he was in a fight for his life, he looked up and didn't see anything. The night-vision goggles had been knocked off his head, and his eyes weren't adjusting to the darkness. They now had the advantage, as he was used to looking at a bright green environment.

He could hear people walking around and speaking, but none of the voices were English. One of the voices standing nearby was Arabic. It was an angry-sounding voice and it was directly over the top of him. It was dark, so Mitchell remained still and slowly prepared his rifle for one last attack. He pointed it in the direction of the Iraqi and pulled the trigger several times.

He stood up to run, but tripped over a fallen Marine. It was the radioman. Next to him was the team leader. He felt his way up the man's body and took the night-vision goggles off his head and held them up to his face. The explosions outside had not subsided, which told Mitchell the fight was still on.

Inside the house, Mitchell saw the insurgent he'd shot. He was leaning against a wall and he was alone. He removed the Ka-Bar he had attached to his belt and silently ran up to the man, stabbing him in the chest. After the blade sank into the man, he began to fight back. Having to defend himself, Darrick dropped the night-vision goggles to pull the knife out of the man's chest. After that, he sliced the man's throat. The insurgent stopped fighting to use both hands in a futile attempt to stop or slow the bleeding. In seconds, the man was limp.

Mitchell stood up, grabbing the NVGs as he went. He saw two Marines lying on the floor in another room. He ran to help them, but a mortar round landed. The blast that killed those two Marines rendered

Mitchell unconscious and threw him several yards from the house, ending the botched raid.

The next morning

Muffled sounds filled Mitchell's ears. He tried to move, but his body was in immense pain. Swells of water gently lifted him up and down against the reeds of the Euphrates.

Another muffled sound. This time he could tell it was a voice.

They're coming for me. They're going to kill me. Maybe even torture me.

He was finished. Mitchell counted himself among the dead Marines and was content to know he was going to die with his brothers, but he decided he wasn't going to let them take him alive, so he went to reach for his rifle. He was going to shoot himself to save himself. The rifle was gone. His mind was still in a fog. Mitchell knew the worst possible fate was about to befall him. Too painful to move. Too weak to fight. One of the men grabbed him. More muffled voices. His eyes were blurry and his head was aching.

Mitchell was placed on a rescue stretcher and evacuated on foot. His vision was starting to return, and he could clearly see Marines to his left and to his right. He didn't recognize any of them. He began to call out the names of those who died in the raid.

"Easy, brother. We got you. You're going home," he heard.

Turning to the voice, Mitchell asked, "Did anybody else make it?"

The Marine didn't answer at first, but Mitchell pressed, "Did anybody else make it?"

"No, man. You're the only one making it out," he finally said.

Mitchell didn't want to make it, though.

How can I live with myself knowing everybody on my team died? Who gets to make that call? Why didn't I die? Those men should have killed me. The mortar should have killed me. I don't want to be alive.

***

"Darrick, you okay?" he heard a feminine voice whisper.

He snapped out of his memory and looked back at Kara. He was back at the Berts' homestead with Kara. She was looking at him with concern written all over her face.

"Are you okay?" she asked a second time.

"I'm good. Stay down. I'm going to clear the house. After that, we collect Jimmie."

Kara nodded to him. She watched as Darrick pulled the door open and entered. It was a well maneuvered and quick entry. She was impressed. It would have gone down perfectly except for that delay where he seemed to be out of it. After about five minutes, she began to grow concerned.

I hope he's alright.

About that time, Darrick came walking around from the rear corner of the house. "All clear."

Kara stepped out from the rabbit cages and began walking toward the area where Jimmie's body was located. "He's over here."

Darrick joined her as she began stepping into the woods.

"He's here," she said, locating him.

Darrick took one look at Jimmie and began to break down. His eyes were hazy white and lifeless. Other parts of his body looked as if they had been chewed up by wild predators.

Kara caressed his shoulder. "Are you sure you want to do this?" she asked in a soft tone.

"Have to. We can't leave him out here like those two idiots," he said, pointing at Larry and Shawn, who appeared to be in better condition than Jimmie. Perhaps due to the location of the bodies.

"I'll go get some bed linens out of the house and a couple of two-by-fours out of the barn. We can make a stretcher," she said.

Darrick nodded in agreement and sat with Jimmie as Kara left them alone together.

Jimmie was still wearing their dad's analogue Timex wristwatch. When he went to remove the family heirloom from his wrist, he began to cry again. Jimmie's hand was cold, and rigor mortis had long since set in. He removed the watch and placed it on his own wrist. It was to serve him as a reminder of due diligence and rational forethought. Jimmie had lost his life because he believed Darrick's word that he was going to check on the Berts. That lie exacted a heavy price. Darrick realized the only person to blame was himself. The guilt was weighing upon him. He acted mad at Kara for not telling him about his brother, but even that was his fault. He wouldn't even be dead if he hadn't lied and went out on his own.

Darrick placed his right hand on Jimmie's chest and said, "I'm so sorry, Jimmie."

A noise came from the north. Darrick looked up and out of the woods to see Kara bringing the items they needed to make a hasty stretcher. She carried them into the woods and set the three items to the left side of Jimmie's body.

"Thanks," he said.

Kara spread a light blanket out onto the ground and laid the two-by-fours on top of it about a foot and half apart. After that, she folded the ends of the blanket back over the top of the boards with one end lying under the other.

"Ready to put him on?" she asked.

"Yeah, let's do this."

They stood up together and grabbed Jimmie by the clothes he was wearing to move him onto the stretcher. Jimmie's body was lying on the blanket that was folded over onto itself. His weight kept the blanket in place so that they could grab the boards and lift him up and out of the woods.

Kara was staying quiet. She was feeling uneasy about saying anything at all. The entire moment was a solemn event. She refused to break the silence, feeling that it wasn't her place.

***

Three men were scouting an area a few short miles from the Omen's center of operation. It was a quiet, routine maneuver until one of them began to hear voices.

The group of three was being led by a military veteran familiar with tactical operations, specifically, hand signs. He threw up a fist, signaling to the two men behind him that they needed to stop moving.

"Do you guys hear that?" the group leader asked.

The other two men stood very still and listened.

"I hear movement in the woods just ahead," the second man in line whispered.

They waited another minute or two.

"I don't hear anything," the third man said.

"Go prone," the leader said, using only a hand signal.

Both men lay down on the ground while the leader moved as quietly through the woods as he could. The sounds he was following abated, so he stood still and went back to listening.

Nothing. He continued out of sheer curiosity and came to an old farmhouse. There were two dead men and a dead woman lying outside. He recognized one of the deceased men and slowly approached him. It was Larry Upton, one of the missing scouts. The leader pulled his rifle into his shoulder and put it in the high ready position, expecting trouble. He pointed it at the window of the house, expecting the moment to erupt into gunfire, but it didn't happen. He walked toward the house. The back door was wide open, but it was also dead silent. He crept ever so silently up to the door and entered with tactical precision.

So far, so good.

The man cleared the front two rooms and moved to the hallway, where he found the body of another man he identified as Shawn Hillerman. The dead scout had a bullet hole in his head, and the carpet beneath him was saturated.

He knelt down to touch it.

Still wet.

He moved on to the next two rooms.

Empty.

He turned around and headed for the front room. When he reached it, he used the tip of his rifle barrel to open the curtain and look outside. He saw two people. A man and a woman. They were carrying what appeared to be an injured person on a stretcher. All three of them were headed away from the ranch.

The man ran out the back door and headed for his teammates.

***

"They've been gone a long time," Carissa said to Tonya.

"They'll be here," Tonya answered, being careful not to make any promises the way she had before, when Darrick let them down.

Carissa had been standing at the kitchen window for the past hour and hadn't sat down or quit squirming.

"You need to relax," Tonya insisted, but Carissa wasn't hearing it.

"I'll relax when my Jimmie comes home," she said. As if on cue, she saw Darrick and Kara in the distance. She ran out the back door without telling Tonya what she was doing. Tonya chased her outside and saw her running toward Darrick and Kara. They were carrying a stretcher with Jimmie's body. It was covered with a blanket.

Carissa met them at the edge of the yard. Darrick and Kara lowered the stretcher to the ground.

"Carissa," Darrick said.

She dropped to her knees at Jimmie's side and placed one hand on Jimmie's head. Darrick was worried that she would attempt to uncover him. He knew that his condition was bad and didn't want her to see his face.

Carissa began to wail, and the sound of it made Darrick's eyes well up with tears. He was about to break and didn't want the women to see him cry, so he left their presence and walked toward the back door, where Tonya was standing. He grabbed her by the hand and led her to the couch, where he sat down, and she sat next to him.

He started to cry. It wasn't a loud *I want to be heard* cry, but rather it was a soft concealed mourning. His eyes and nose filled with tears. Tonya listened to him sniff and exhale his anguish as he tried to conceal his face from her. She pulled him in for a hug and let him cry on her shoulder. This was the second time Tonya ever saw Darrick cry. The first time was when he first told her about his childhood trauma. Tonya didn't believe it was the trauma of being beaten with metal clothes hangers that made him cry, but the thought of having lost a father in the process. It was the loss that had driven Darrick to tears.

Now, with Jimmie gone, she was seeing his pain come alive again for the second time. His loss was felt by her and she joined him in tears. When he had made an end to his evening's mourning, he stood up from Tonya's side and said, "I guess I need to get him buried." Darrick thought for a moment. "I know just the place."

Across the street from the homestead, there were a few acres of land that the Mitchells used to small-game hunt. There was a glade about a half mile away. Darrick used to hide there when he was young. It was the only place he felt both alone and safe. *That would be a great spot to bury him,* he thought.

Just outside the homestead on the nearest hill

The scouts who found Larry and Shawn had just lain down on the ground at the crest of the closest hill. The leader of the trio had a pair of binoculars in hand. He was intently watching the scene unfold just on the edge of the upkept portion of the yard.

"I see two women now. One of them is the lady I saw back at the ranch. The other one is crying pretty heavy. She must be the wife or girlfriend of the person on the stretcher. I don't see the man anymore," the leader said. "No, wait," he said. "The man is coming back out of the house, and it looks like they're moving the body of the person on the stretcher. Maybe to go bury him."

"Should we take 'em?" the second man asked.

"No, Carl, we shouldn't *take 'em*," he replied with a cynical tone. "We're going to wait here and scout. Not act irrational. Let them bury their dead in peace. When we know more, we'll take reasonable action."

"But this could be the man who killed Larry, Shawn, and probably Max."

"My point exactly. If this is the guy who killed them, then we need to act responsibly and avoid certain death. Don't you think so, Carl?"

"Good point."

The man with the binoculars looked at the third man and said, "Russell, can you go scout a good spot for us to safely pitch for this evening?"

"No problem."

The man backed down off the hill, leaving the leader and Carl alone together. Once Russell was far enough away, the leader looked at Carl and said, "I swear to God, if you do anything to compromise my life, I will kill you myself."

Carl was used to being threatened, but this threat in particular scared him. It was the look in the man's eyes that frightened him. "I won't do anything to place us in danger, Mark. I promise."

Later that night

The chickens started clucking as three armed men crept silently alongside the coop. The moon was subdued with clouds, and the refracted light was barely enough to silhouette objects on the ground. The sudden sound startled them. They frantically moved away from the chickens, hoping to bring their incessant cackling to a halt.

"They have chickens," Carl said.

"Shut up, Carl!"

Carl had a knack for stating the obvious. The other two loved the fact that they could crack *Carl jokes* about him. Carl didn't seem to understand the humor behind it. He was a short bald man with a full beard and mustache. He was overly hairy on every inch of his body except for his head, which had a remarkable resistance to sunburn.

"I haven't had chicken in weeks," Carl whispered.

"Shut up, Carl," Russell whispered. "You're going to get us shot."

Mark and Russell couldn't see Carl's face in the dark, but he was scowling at them. He hated it when they told him to shut up. Undoubtedly, Carl was told to shut up more than anybody he knew.

"Russ," Mark said, capturing his attention, "there's way too much cloud cover. We don't have enough light to safely maneuver."

Russell was a medium-built man with a taste for tobacco and was known to trade almost anything for a dip or a cigarette. Two years after the Pulse made tobacco products hard to come by, he was willing to make high-stakes bargains for something so rare.

"What do you recommend?" Russell asked. Before Mark could reply, he heard crunching sounds.

Crunch, crunch, crunch.

Both Russell and Mark looked over in Carl's direction. He was chewing on something that might not have been so loud if not for it being the dead of night in a valley.

Click, click, Todd and Carl heard.

Mark had his pistol out and pointing at Carl's head. Carl felt the cool steel press against his temple. He kept chewing like he had to finish a task he had started.

"If you get me shot, you'll be dead before me. Do I make myself clear?" Mark said.

"Perfectly," Carl replied with a mouthful of peanuts.

Mark uncocked his pistol and put it away.

"Don't be burning through our resources, Carl," Todd said, smelling the peanuts on his breath.

"Let's get outta here," Mark said, turning to leave the area. "We can come back as soon as we can see. Carl, you've got first watch."

Carl and Russell followed close behind Mark.

The next morning
August 15th

Mark was up before the break of dawn. He left Russell and Carl to go stake out the property on his own, not being completely confident in his team. The house had plenty of blind spots that he thought he would remove if he were the one in charge of it. But for now, he thought to himself, *There's wooded areas, an old car with overgrowth, a barn, all of which are viable positions to take cover and watch from a reasonable distance.*

He began to make his way closer to the house, being careful to note any indications as to how many people were living at the homestead. He was moving from one concealed location to another, making mental notes as he progressed.

Okay, first glance, recent deconstruction on the barn reveals that they are actively trying to hide their location.

Chickens! Chickens are a smart sustainable food source that can provide both meat and eggs.

An underground well.

Toys! They have at least one child.

Peanuts! Peanuts? Carl!

Mark was livid. Carl had left evidence of their visit last night. Fortunately, it appeared as though it had not yet been discovered. No sooner than he reached down to collect the evidence, he heard the back door of the house as it was opening. He rapidly withdrew his extended arm and hid himself.

Darrick stepped outside to survey the land. It was a routine of his to make sure things were the way he'd left them. The security of the homestead was of the utmost importance. Especially because they had recently been discovered by three men, all of whom he'd had to neutralize. He gazed around the backyard and saw that everything seemed to be in order. As he was turning to reenter the house, he saw the chickens were scattering. He froze. His eyes began searching the area, looking for something out of the ordinary. He listened intently.

Somebody's here.

He backed toward the door and reached out for the handle, never taking his eyes off the environment near the chicken coop. He could see a pair of boots under the wooden table structure that was between the back door and pen.

Mark was crouched down, looking through a crack in the structure at the man he'd tracked the previous day from the ranch house. He felt a surge of adrenaline shoot through his veins, and his heart began to pound deeply.

I think he sees me, he thought, being careful not to move an inch.

Darrick remained frozen as he considered his next move. He wanted to run at the intruder, but he had no idea whether or not the stranger was armed. He couldn't see anything but men's boots on the ground, not enough to make a sound decision. He finally decided to err on the side of caution and reenter the house. Grabbing a weapon would be priority one. Once he reached the door and the handle was firmly grasped, he stepped into the house and locked the door behind him.

"Tonya," he called out. She was still asleep in the front room with Kara and Andy.

"Tonya," he called out again, this time running into the front room and grabbing a rifle. "There's a man out back," he said.

Kara quit rubbing her eyes and shot up off her end of the couch.

"Let's go," Darrick said, kicking the sleeping Tonya in the feet. No sooner than she was startled awake, he said, "Lock this behind me," and he stormed out the front door.

"What's going on?" Tonya said, standing up from the couch.

"I think he said something about a man outside," Kara answered. She was already grabbing a rifle. Andy was still sound asleep, oblivious to all the noise and slamming doors. "I got this," Kara said. "Take Andy upstairs and tell Carissa what's going on."

Tonya scooped the sleeping lad up into her arms, barely able to lift the deadweight, and headed up the stairs.

A few moments later

"Get up," Mark said, grabbing a backpack from the ground and throwing it at Carl. "Somebody's coming." .

Russell sat up. "Did you say somebody was coming?"

Mark was frantically stuffing his sleeping gear into the backpack.

"You went off without us, didn't you?" Russell said as he joined Mark in packing their belongings.

"I didn't want to risk being seen," Mark said, trying to explain his actions.

"Well, so much for that."

"Just pack up. I've yet to see more than one man. I suspect he'll be coming over that hill real soon, so I think we should head in that direction over there and avoid the conflict altogether."

Russell looked at Carl and then back to Mark.

"Let me get this right," Russell said, dropping his pack and grabbing his rifle. "*You* want to avoid a confrontation?"

"That's right," Mark answered without hesitation.

Mark finished packing his bag and threw it over his shoulders. "I scoped the place out, and there's no evidence that these people had anything to do with the deaths of Larry and Shawn."

"I'm not buying it," Russell rebutted. "We tracked the man from Larry and Shawn's bodies to this house and you're saying he had nothing to do with it."

"No, I said there's no evidence that they had anything to do with it." Mark began walking away.

"We're not allowed to split up, Mark. If Denver finds out you abandoned us, he'll kill you."

"Only if you tell him I abandoned you, Russell," Mark turned to say.

Russell looked at Carl and said, "I'm not leaving until we find what we're looking for. Mark would be wise not to return to the Enclave without us. I say we leave our stuff here and ambush the man when he arrives."

Carl hadn't said a word since he'd been awake. He simply grabbed his rifle and took a position in some foliage. Russell did the same. They waited.

Darrick stopped well short of their position and took his time scouting out the area.

I wish I would have brought my pack.

He had run off in such a hurry that he completely forgot to grab some essentials. He lowered his body and assumed a prone position, which he used to inch his way to the crestline of a hill. Once he broke the horizon, he knew he was at risk of being seen. Without binoculars, he would have to rely on his eyesight. The day was young and the sun was casting long shadows, making it difficult to see things that were out of the ordinary. One thing stood out. Amidst the broken colors, foliage, and overgrowth, Darrick saw a solid olive drab-colored one-man tent out in the open. He figured it belonged to the intruder.

I don't see anybody.

He looked long and hard, but there was no movement until something out of the corner of his eye caught his attention. He was too late.

Busted!

"No sudden movements, pal," a man said from behind him.

Darrick offered up no preemptive cooperation. *If this guy wants me to let go of my gun, it's not going to happen.*

"Let go of the rifle and scoot backwards, nice and slow."

Russell was standing over Darrick with his rifle pointed squarely at him.

I think I can take him, Darrick thought.

Russell looked out over Darrick toward Carl's position and waved him in. Darrick was strongly considering a fight until he saw the big burly man come out from the green foliage and start his ascent to their position on the hill. He knew he could take one armed idiot who was standing over him, but not two, even if he had the elevation advantage. Too much could go wrong.

"I'm not telling you again, pal. Let go of the rifle," Russell said. When the man on the ground didn't cooperate, he hit him on the back of the head with the buttstock of his rifle.

***

"Open the door," a husky male voice demanded. The command was followed by four heavy pounds on the back door of the house.

Carissa was awake by now and looking to Kara, hoping that she might find the voice familiar. Tonya and Andy were still upstairs. Andy was shown where to hide again, and Tonya stayed with elder Mitchell. Turned out, she reminded him of his deceased wife, giving her an ability nobody else had: she could get him to cooperate if she used a sweet voice to do it.

Kara shrugged her shoulders at Carissa and mouthed, "I don't know," to her. Carissa was terrified. Darrick was gone and a stranger was beating on the back door. Both of them grabbed a rifle and headed for the kitchen. Carissa peeked through the back-window curtains and saw a stranger. In the background, on the wooden table structure, Darrick was tied down, and there was a second man with a rifle pointed at Darrick's head. His finger was on the trigger. Carissa didn't recognize the man at the door or the man who had Darrick at gunpoint.

The man at the door was Russell, but the ladies of the Mitchell homestead didn't know him.

"You know this man?" Russell asked with an authoritative voice.

"What do you want?" Carissa answered with a question of her own.

"I'm the one in charge now, woman! Open this door right now or my friend will pull the trigger on ol' boy's head."

Carissa looked at Kara. "What do we do?" she mouthed.

Kara knew they had them trapped for action.

"Is there anything we can do?" Kara mouthed back.

Carissa was overwhelmed with anxiety and confusion over the situation. She couldn't make out what Kara said. Just before she could ask her to repeat herself, there was a loud bash to the door and it flew open, breaking the frame where the lock bolted in.

In response, Carissa pointed the rifle and pulled the trigger. The man was in the process of charging into the room when he heard the gun go off. It stopped him dead in his tracks. He groped his abdomen, expecting to see blood or feel some kind of pain, but there was nothing. She'd missed completely.

Russell looked over his shoulder at Carl and Darrick. When he did that, it reminded Carissa exactly how high the stakes were. Had they been given more time to plan, Kara supposed she might have left out the front door and jumped the men from behind. But all that was behind them now. The man with a gun on Darrick hadn't pulled the trigger yet.

The man in the doorway pulled his rifle up. "Easy there, pretty lady. My buddy over there's got a rifle on that man's head. All I have to do is give the word and, *boom,* he's dead. Do you understand?"

"What do you want?" Carissa asked.

"I'm looking for a friend. A man by the name of Max. I think you might know where he is or maybe have some information for me."

Carissa shook her head.

"Is that a no, as in *no, you're not going to help me,* or a no, as in *no, you don't know*?"

"We don't know nobody by the name of Max around here," Carissa answered.

Russell looked over her and glared at Kara. "What about you? You were there. You were there with that man on the table out there where I found my dead friends, Larry Upton and Shawn Hillerman."

"We were looking for Jimmie Mitchell," Kara answered. "We found him dead with your friends. We figured they killed each other. We brought Jimmie home. The rest is history."

***

Upstairs, Andy was doing his best to remain silent and still, but elder Mitchell didn't have it in him to do the same. The crashing sound of the door startled him from his sleep.

"Shhh," Tonya said to elder Mitchell. She was trying to hold him down with one hand and keep her hand over his mouth with the other, but the whole thing only caused more confusion in the old man's mind.

When he finally could break away from her, he punched her in the face and charged out the door.

***

Russell heard a loud noise coming from the upstairs. "Who else is here?" asked, withdrawing toward the exit.

Kara seized the moment and yelled, "Roy, Bob, Tommy, get down here now!" Of course, she completely made the names up on the fly, hoping to frighten the intruder out of the house. Her plan worked.

Russell shot out the back door and headed toward Carl and Darrick. He ducked behind the yard table and pointed his rifle at the back door, fully expecting to see men running out. When that didn't happen, Russell knew he had been duped.

Just on the other side of the kitchen door, elder Mitchell was storming into the kitchen. "What's all this ruckus?"

"James, you need to go back upstairs," Carissa said, pushing him back through the corridor that led to the front room.

Tonya came running down the stairs. She was holding her face where he'd punched her. "Come on, James," Tonya said, but he wasn't having it.

"I demand to know what this ruckus is all about!" He looked at the door frame and saw that it was shattered around the locking mechanism. "What did you do now, Pudge?" He tried to push through Tonya, but Kara joined in to help restrain him.

The back door pushed open again, and Russell aimed his rifle sights on Kara. "That was a bad idea, woman," the intruder said.

Kara had a rifle, but it was at her side. Helping control elder Mitchell took much of her focus. When she looked back and saw the man had a rifle pointed at her, she let go of elder Mitchell.

James looked at the man and said, "What'd you do, Pudge? Look at that door! What'd you do?"

Carissa used the distraction to her advantage and pointed her rifle at Russell. He grabbed the barrel end and jerked it out of her hands. By that time, elder Mitchell was making his approach on Russell. He was just within arm's reach when Russell backhanded the elderly man and knocked him down. He then used the stock end of the rifle to strike Carissa in the abdomen. The pain was excruciating. She bowed over and winced. When she did, Russell pulled her in and held her between himself and the rifle that Kara was now pointing at him.

"That was some ninja-like footwork, right!" Russell said with a tone of excitement. "By now, I'm guessing all the help you have in this house is an old man on the floor, a pretty girl in my arms, that unarmed woman right there, and you!"

Kara took a survey of the environment and realized she had no viable options.

"On the couch, both of you," Russell commanded.

Kara lowered the rifle to the floor. Both she and Tonya moved around the outside of the room and made their way to the couch. Russell threw Carissa between them. They all sat down.

"Everything alright in there, Russ?" Carl yelled from outside.

Knowing that he had the women in control and the old man was out like a light, Russell yelled back, "Come in here, Carl."

Carl nervously entered the house. Russell saw how apprehensive he was acting. "Knock it off, doughboy. This is everybody."

Carl looked at the women. He pointed at Kara. "That's the one we followed."

"Shut up, Carl," Russell said. "God, I want to shoot you myself. Why do you always have to be so rhetorical?"

"What's rhetorical?"

"Shut up, Carl! Head back to the Enclave and make sure Rueben knows we found Larry, Shawn, and possibly Max. Ask him what he wants us to do with them. Tell him they killed our people."

"Did they tell you where Max is?" he asked.

"Carl! Head back and do what I said."

"But are we for sure they killed Shawn, Larry, and Max, or are we just going off a hunch?"

"Think *extra rations*, Carl. That should motivate you."

Carl frowned at Russell and said, "You know Denver don't want us to separate. You're making me no better than Mark."

Russell rolled his eyes and Carl left.

Turning his attention back to the women on the couch, he said, "I'm only going to ask once. After that, I shoot one of you. If you don't talk after that, I shoot another, and on and on until I run out of people to shoot."

Tonya, Kara, and Carissa were sitting silently, each of them wondering who would be the first to speak.

"Where's Max?"

Tonya began to cry. Carissa was all cried out, and Kara was just too jaded to care.

"Your men, Larry and Shawn, held me captive for days," Kara answered. "They raped me, tortured me, and hid me from the Enclave for fear of being killed for their lusts."

The answer surprised and shocked Russell. He was taken aback by the information. "So where's Max?"

"I don't know where Max went. When he shot and killed my partner, they took me and tied me up to a tree while they murdered those old folks at that ranch where we found Jimmie. They came back for me. After that, they kept me in a closet like a wild animal and fed me scraps. Just enough to keep me alive. They left together to do some more scouting, but only Shawn and Larry returned. That's all I know." Kara was hoping the man would be appeased and let them go, but that was a pipe dream.

"You were there," Russell said. "You were there, so you know who killed them. They deserved what they had coming if what you say is true. But I gotta know. Who killed them?"

Kara thought for a moment before deciding her own fate. When she was at peace with her decision, she answered the man. "I killed them. I killed Russell and Shawn." Of course, she was lying. The answer she decided to give their captive was thoroughly thought out. Right down to the detail. "Shawn came in to rape me. I escaped the knot he tied. He was wearing a gun. I killed him with it. Then I went outside and killed Larry."

Russell considered all the information she had provided. He spent about thirty seconds scratching his scalp and running his fingers through his thin beard. "You know, it almost makes sense. Except it doesn't. Shawn was shot in the back of the head. Larry was shot in the back of the head. Can you explain to me how two men get shot in the back of the head? Don't you think the first shot would alert the other man? I'm not buying your story. Now, I followed you back from that ranch house, and you were with that man," Russell said, pointing to the backyard, when he had a thought.

I'll just torture the man until he confesses and tells us where Max is.

Russell looked around and saw some backpacks lying around on the floor. He walked over to the closest pack and knelt next to it, never taking his eyes off the women. With one hand on the rifle and the other on the pack, he began to rummage around inside it. "I know you got some rope in one of these packs," he said. "I mean, who doesn't keep rope in a bugout bag?"

The women remained silent.

When he didn't find what he was looking for in that pack, he grabbed the next one. "Looky-looky," he said, pulling out fifty feet of paracord. He threw it at Tonya, the woman he perceived to be the weakest among them, and said, "Tie 'em up, now."

Tonya had the rope in her hands when she turned to look at Kara and Carissa. Kara was expressionless, but Carissa was shaking her head. "No."

Russell ran up to Carissa, grabbing her by the hair and throwing her on the ground. When he did, Tonya and Kara stood up in preparation to charge at their captor, but he pointed his rifle at them and said, "Nuh-uh."

They stopped dead in their tracks.

Carissa already had one arm in a backpack that she was familiar with. She pulled out a pocketknife and quietly opened it. Russell had no sooner turned around than he was met with a stab to the upper pectoral muscle just under his left shoulder. He yelled and punched Carissa to the floor. He pulled the knife out of his chest and was making his way to Carissa.

Elder Mitchell was making his way to his feet, and Russell heard it. He kicked Carissa unconscious and turned around to deal with the old man. Both Kara and Tonya were back on their feet.

Russell wrangled elder Mitchell into a choke hold, using the rifle for leverage. It was clear that the old man was no match for the much younger and stronger aggressor. "I'm done with the lot of you!" Russell said, choking the life out of his elderly victim. "Who's gonna miss an old fart?" he taunted as he pulled the rifle in tight against James's neck.

Elder Mitchell's knees were giving out and his arms were going limp when the sound of a gunshot went off. A pink mist flew out of Russell's head and splattered over Carissa's unconscious body. Russell let go of elder Mitchell and they both fell limp to the ground.

There was a dead silence. Then a kitchen floorboard creaked.

Kara and Tonya remained frozen.

"Tonya," a voice called out from the kitchen. Kara didn't recognize the man's voice, but Tonya did. She jumped up and ran to the middle of the floor, stepping over Russell's body.

"Marcus?" Tonya asked, looking at Marcus Guy, also known as *Mark*, Darrick's military buddy.

"Come on," Marcus said. "We don't have time."

"Time for what? What's going on?"

"There's a man on his way back to the Enclave. If they find out you're here and believe that you had anything to do with the deaths of their people, you'll all be cleansed."

"Marcus, I don't understand," she said. Kara and Carissa were helping elder Mitchell to his feet.

Marcus took one more look at her before heading out the back door and saying, "There's no time to explain. Get out of the area. Head west if possible. Stay away from the crows and you'll be fine."

"Crows?" Tonya asked.

Marcus didn't stick around. He ran out the door, right past Darrick's unconscious body, and off the property toward Carl.

"Tonya, who was that?" Kara asked.

"It's a long, long story," she replied, still confused from her encounter. Kara shot out the door to where Darrick was tied down and began releasing him.

When Tonya saw that Kara was being more attentive to her husband than she was, she ran out to assist. "Wake up, hon," Tonya said, jiggling Darrick's cheeks. He was out cold.

Carissa ran out the door to the water well and drew up a bucket of water. She carried it over to Darrick and dumped it over his face, waking him from his sleep.

Darrick was dazed and confused. There was some dried blood mingled with new blood on the back of Darrick's head. It was apparent from that and the lump that he had been hit hard. Darrick grabbed his head and squeezed his eyes shut. "Oh God, my head is killing me."

"You've been hit pretty hard in the head," Kara said, gently touching his scalp where he was hit.

Tonya's jealousy was growing. She pushed herself between Darrick and Kara. "Let's get you in and cleaned up," Tonya said. "Can you get another bucket of water, Carissa?" Tonya asked, helping Darrick off the table.

Tonya walked with Darrick into the house, leaving Kara and Carissa outside, where they began whispering.

"Are we going to completely ignore the strange man who burst in here and saved us?" Kara asked.

"I know, right? Tonya knew him by name!"

"And what was that stuff about the crows and being cleansed?"

"I don't know, but it was creepy."

In the house, Tonya was sitting next to Darrick and elder Mitchell on the couch. James wasn't acting like himself. Darrick and Tonya both noticed that he was gazing off into the distance like he was watching something far away.

Not paying much attention to the dead man on the floor, Darrick noticed his dad. "What's up with him?"

"That guy choked him half to death," Tonya said, pointing to Russell's lifeless corpse.

"Which one of you had the pleasure of shooting him?" he asked, nodding to the dead man.

"It was me," Tonya said, looking over Darrick's shoulder toward the kitchen door, where Kara and Carissa were standing in awe of Tonya's blatant lie.

They glared at her, Darrick not knowing that there was an unspoken contention brewing between Kara, Carissa, and Tonya. Tonya had her eyes locked onto each of them and was slowly shaking her head back and forth, signaling that they not reveal the truth to Darrick. All Kara and Carissa could do was look at each other. They were deeply confused over Tonya's intentions.

"You don't expect me to believe that, do you?" Darrick asked. Both Kara and Carissa looked back at Tonya, believing she had been busted. Darrick looked at her too. Her face was reddening. When Darrick saw it, he said, "I mean, you couldn't kill a bug. So who really killed him?"

Tonya's mouth was open, but no words were being said.

"I did," Carissa said, stepping forward into the picture. "Why'd you tell him you shot him, Tonya?" Carissa had found a way to both call Tonya out on her lie and to cover for her. Kara was still perplexed and unwilling to play along.

"I, uh, I thought he'd be upset knowing the truth," Tonya said, outwitting her.

Carissa thought for a moment. "You should have informed me first before deciding on your own that you wanted to hide something from your husband."

"Where's the other guy?" Darrick said, interrupting them.

Kara, Carissa, and Tonya knew the other guy had been ordered to return to some place called the Enclave and speak to a man named Rueben. Knowing Tonya was hiding something they didn't know about, they played coy.

"He ran off," Tonya said.

Darrick stood up. "I have to go find him."

"You can't," Tonya said, grabbing him by the arm.

"Why not?"

"He left more than an hour ago. There's no way you'll find him."

Kara was by no means a fighter. She had little to no experience with guns or knives, but she was the most jaded of the three women. Seeing Carissa and Tonya lie to Darrick for reasons she didn't know made her feel uncomfortable. Her career prior to the Pulse had been one of encouraging couples and individuals to be honest and truthful. She had her own issues that she had to deal with from time to time, but in the end, she would be honest. Sitting with people for hour-long sessions meant listening to her clients. There were some occasions in her individualized casework where speaking the truth would cause more harm than good. Kara's strength was knowing how to weigh the balance of honesty against omission. She never lied. When the truth would cause pain or aggravate situations, then she resorted to secrecy. The events that were unfolding in the Mitchell house were against her better judgment, but she knew she didn't have all the available information at hand to make a choice between truth or omission. So she not only excluded herself from the conversation they were having, but she also backed out of the house and quietly left. Of course, she made sure she was equipped with at least a pistol.

Several minutes later
Somewhere east of the Mitchell homestead

"Hey, wait up," Kara called out to Marcus. He was several yards ahead of her. She had practically run to catch up with him. He heard her voice and turned around. Kara was caught off guard when she saw he pulled his pistol out when he whipped around to face her.

"Easy, dude!" she said, putting her hands up in the air.

"What do you want?"

"Just answers," she said.

"I don't have time for this. I've gotta catch up to Carl before he makes his way back to the Enclave."

"What happens if he gets there before you?"

Ignoring her question, Marcus turned around and continued his fast-paced walk toward the Enclave's campsite. There were too many things he needed to have kept quiet. He wasn't about to tell his secrets to a stranger, but if there was anything Kara was good at, it was getting people to open up.

"Are you a friend of Darrick and Tonya?" she asked.

"Listen, lady," Marcus said, stopping mid-stride to turn around and confront her. "I'm about to do something dangerous. It's going to put me in harm's way and it's sure to get you killed. My recommendation to you is to turn around and go make sure Darrick and Tonya get off that property. With any luck, I might be able to buy them some time." Marcus turned back around and picked up his pace.

"I know what happened to your missing men," Kara said, hoping to stop Marcus in his tracks. It worked. Marcus stopped and spun around, but this time, it was Kara who had the drop on him.

"I'm listening," Marcus said, seeing her with a pistol pointed at him.

"I'm not interested in hurting you, but I am interested in making sure nothing happens to Darrick."

"You have a thing for him, don't you?"

"Let me help you stop this Carl guy. We can do it together and maybe give Darrick more than just *time*."

"Fine," he said, conceding to her will. "But you can't follow me into camp. Women aren't allowed to scout, so it'll be an instant red flag if they see me bringing you in."

Kara put her pistol away. Marcus turned to finish his walk. "We'll be lucky if we can catch up to him before he reaches camp," he said.

"If we catch up, what happens?"

"I'm going to try to convince him that you guys had nothing to do with the killing of Shawn and Larry. By the way, what happened to Max?"

"I don't know the details, but he must've given Darrick some hassle on his property, because he killed him," she answered. She was still pondering Marcus's involvement in Tonya's life and why Tonya lied to Darrick about him, so she posed a question of her own. "It's my turn. How do you know Darrick?" she asked. Kara purposefully asked a loaded question. It was obvious that he knew Tonya, but she was curious what he had to hide.

"I was in the Marines with Darrick," he answered.

"That's it? You were in the Marines with him?"

"Yeah, that's it."

"You know as well as I do that's not it. You walked right by Darrick when he was lying on that table back at the farm, not one time, but two times, and you left him there unconscious."

"You really should mind your own business, woman."

"Kara."

"What?"

"My name's Kara."

"Look, Kara. The friendship between me and Darrick is complicated. You would be doing him a favor if you didn't mention me or even let him know that I'm in the area."

"Why, did something happen?"

Marcus stopped and grabbed Kara by the head. He placed one hand over her mouth and the other hand behind her head, pulling her down to the ground behind a tree. "Shhh," he whispered. "It's Carl, up ahead." Marcus released his hold on her, and she held her silence, lying low on the ground. "Stay here," he whispered.

Carl was urinating with his back to Marcus.

"There you are," Marcus called out, startling Carl.

"You skeered the ever-living daylights outta me, Mark."

"Sorry, man."

Carl was putting himself away and wiping the urine from his hands onto his jeans. "All this because you wanted to get a laugh outta me, eh?" Carl said, looking back over Marcus's shoulder. "Where's Russell?"

"Russell got mad at me and said he was done."

"Done? Done with what?"

"Done with the Enclave, man. We had an argument about the people at that farmhouse, and he didn't like what I had to say, so he left. He had a few choice words, but that's all there was to it."

Carl thought the story sounded shady, but he couldn't stand Russell, so he was glad to hear that he wasn't going to be around to belittle him anymore.

"Do you think Ten-Stitches's gonna buy that story?" Carl asked.

The question was enough to let Marcus know that Carl was believing it.

"Carl, those people are good people. They didn't have anything to do with the deaths of our guys. We need to leave them alone."

"I can handle it if they killed Max, or even Russell. Those guys had it coming, but Larry and Shawn? They treated me good. They stuck up for me when people messed with me."

"So what now?" Marcus asked.

"I can't believe it!"

"What?"

"You're actually asking me for my opinion?"

"Shut up, Carl!"

"That's more like it." Carl and Marcus started heading back to the campsite. "I guess we tell him your story, Mark. He got mad at your decision and ran off."

"Okay, so we have an understanding?" Marcus asked.

"Yeah, man. Don't sweat it."

Mitchell Homestead

Tonya was careful to make sure elder Mitchell was removed from the front room scene where Russell had been shot. Carissa cleaned up the blood while Darrick regained his composure. When he felt himself again, he picked up Russell's body from the front porch, where Carissa had dumped him, and took him across the street, to the glade where he had buried Max's body. Andy had come down from his hiding spot nearly an hour ago. He seemed unmindful of the bloodstains that his aunt Carissa was trying fervently to clean.

"Andy, hon, have you seen Kara?" Carissa asked.

Andy shook his head and went back to playing with his Hot Wheels.

She sighed, thinking, *How did I get stuck cleaning this up by myself?*

MEMORIES FROM THE GLADE – MICE AND MEN

The Glade
Mitchell Homestead
August 16th

Darrick sat on the side of a hole that he'd dug into the earth. Just across from him, on the other side of the hole, lay Russell's body. Darrick didn't even know his name. To Darrick, he was a violent man who deserved no kind words, no memorial service, no anything. Just a cold, empty, unmarked shallow grave. Darrick believed he got what he had coming to him. Russell was the fourth man to be killed in recent days and the second man killed in the Mitchell home in as many days. Darrick was already tired of burying bodies and was hoping that the violence was over.

Across the glade, Darrick could see Jimmie's grave. It was marked with a decorative cross that he'd made from wood he'd taken from the walls of the barn. Although Russell had nothing to do with the death of Jimmie, Darrick had a growing hate for the group he came from. Hearing small talk between the women in the house, he was able to piece together that Russell was from the same group Max was. Also, he was able to figure out that the two men he'd killed at the Berts' house killed Jimmie and were also members of the group he knew only as the

Omen. This knowledge was coalescing in his mind, and he was actively resisting the urge to run off and do something stupid.

Andy needs you in his life. He needs a father figure to teach him manly things. He needs to learn to hunt, make traps, shelters, survive and thrive. Who will be there for him if I run off and do something that could get me killed? What about Tonya? She needs my support, my strength, my skills. Stay focused, Darrick. Stay frosty and stay alive.

Darrick was hot. His energy levels were low. He'd easily burned through all of his calories and sweated out all of his water intake by digging this hole. Even though the shade was plentiful in the glade, the heat index was high. He looked into Russell's lifeless eyes and wished he could access the things he knew about the Omen. There was nothing on him that he could use as a clue. The thought of having no answers to all of his questions only frustrated him more.

When he was finished catching his breath, he stood up and walked around to the back side of Russell's body and stooped down to roll him over into the hole. He was heavy at first, but once the momentum was on his side, the body fell into the pit and made a *thump* as it landed. It was the signal Darrick needed to start filling the pit. Slightly easier than digging, he knew he was over halfway done.

In a way, Darrick loathed filling the pits more than he did digging them. When he was busy digging, he always focused on the work at hand. Filling the pits wasn't much of a bother. It was in those times his mind began to roam. He reminisced. He missed his brother, Jimmie; he thought about the care Tonya needed and the lessons he had yet to teach his son, Andy. He thought about his new friend Kara and his ailing father. It was only a matter of time before he would have to dig another grave and bury another person he cared about.

One thought dominated his mind. It was the understanding that everybody dies – nobody lives forever. Whether he liked it or not, one day he was going to dig a hole for is father, or worse yet, his family would have to dig a hole for him. Darrick Mitchell was going to die. His wife, his son, his friends, and everybody in the world was going to die. So, with such a truth burrowing holes in his mind, how was he to focus on survival? What was the point in fighting and trying to live? Why postpone the inevitable?

Darrick didn't know the answers. He only understood that he had an insatiably strong will to live. His combat training would be used to bring that inevitability to his enemies, and his friends and family would be standing beside him at the end. *Because life and property,* Darrick thought, *are worth fighting for, and nobody's going to destroy what is mine and live to tell the tale.*

SNITCHES END UP IN DITCHES

Enclave Camp

August 15th

Cornelius was leaning against the corner of the barn with his right leg folded over his left and a piece of grass hanging from his lips. He tried to make a habit of making everybody's business his own. When he wasn't sulking in his own thoughts, he would watch others. Cornelius had an understanding that most people in the Enclave did not have. Knowledge is power. Watch people and learn everything you can. You never know when you might need something on someone. Some little piece of dirt, some piece of information might be a treasure trove, and holding it, the power of life and death.

On this particular occasion Cornelius saw Carl and Mark coming back from their scouting routine. But something was different. Russell wasn't there. They knew the rules. Never, never separate from the team. They went out in scouting parties of three people for a reason. They supported each other, they assisted each other, and they made sure they came back with as many people as went out. Here was where Cornelius excelled. He wasn't going to approach the two men. He was going to listen.

"Remember, just stick to the story, and everything will be fine," Mark said.

"I know, I know!" Carl replied. "Russell didn't like what you had to say, so he ran off on his own. There's nothing we can do about that."

Marcus looked up and saw Cornelius leaning against the barn. It was nothing new to them to see him standing there. Everybody thought Cornelius was shady, but they never questioned him. He had Rueben's favor, and to mess with him meant flirting with disaster. Making eye contact with Cornelius caused a nervous sensation to fill Marcus with worry. It was the look that he gave. That cocky "I know something you don't know" look. Marcus ignored it, broke eye contact, and continued on.

Carl followed close behind him, being careful not to make eye contact with anybody. Carl was not a very confident man to begin with. It was especially easy to tell if something was bothering him because of the way he behaved. He would look down, not make eye contact, or excessively scratch his nose.

Marcus and Carl were careful in their approach. Rueben was sitting at a table outside in the shade of one of the corrals. He had his pistol disassembled and a cleaning brush that he was using to scrape off the carbon. There was no cleaning lubricant or gun oil in his possession. So he did what most people did to clean their weapons. He used motor oil. Anything to smooth the operation of the gun was viable. Rueben saw them coming and knew immediately they were one person short. "Where's your third man?"

"Ran into a problem, Rueben."

"What kind of problem?"

"We went searching for Larry, Shawn, and Max. We stumbled on an old farmhouse. They weren't there, but there were some pretty ladies. Russell was looking for action, but I wouldn't have it. We got into an argument, he said he was done with it all, and he left."

"That's it? Just done with it? That doesn't sound like Russell to me."

Carl began scratching his nose. He broke eye contact with Rueben and began to excessively look around the property. Marcus saw what Carl was doing and wanted to choke the life out of him. He saw it as a weakness and wished that he had never brought him along. Now they had this problem and they had to deal with it.

"Weapons check," Rueben said as he reassembled his pistol.

Marcus and Carl began to panic. Marcus's pistol was one bullet short. Scouts were not given extra ammunition. If they had a fifteen-round magazine, they received fifteen rounds. There wasn't one extra for the chamber; there wasn't one extra for good luck. They received exactly the amount, and that was how Rueben was able to micromanage things.

Marcus looked at Rueben and said, "I'm going to be one round short. I had an accidental discharge."

Carl remained silent.

Rueben looked at Marcus with one eyebrow raised. Marcus was careful to look in Rueben's eyes with confidence. Carl could not perform the same. Instead, he was looking around the property, uncomfortable in his own skin.

"You've never given me a reason to doubt your performance, Marcus. I'm going to give you the benefit of the doubt."

Carl seemed excited. He smirked.

Rueben was picking up on the subtle changes in Carl's behavior. He knew he was being deceived, but he was right in believing that Marcus had never done anything to make him question his performance before.

"Rueben, can I talk to you for a moment?" a voice said from the side.

Marcus and Carl looked over in the direction of the voice. It was Cornelius. Marcus remembered making eye contact with him when they entered camp. Marcus was already considering an exit strategy. A plan B, if you will.

Rueben always had three or four men surrounding him. It was his way of showing force and intimidation.

"Keep an eye on them," Rueben ordered. On this particular occasion, Rueben had three armed guards with him, and when Rueben gave the order, the men surrounded both Carl and Marcus. Rueben stepped off to be alone with Cornelius. Marcus was trying to read their lips but he was no good at it. He assumed the worst, and in so doing, he was correct. Cornelius was squealing on them, telling Rueben everything he'd overheard.

The conversation was over. Rueben stepped back over to where Carl and Marcus were standing, and gave his guards the order.

"Take them to the hog trough."

The guards immediately grabbed the weapons from their possession as if they routinely performed the task for Rueben.

It was not the order that either Marcus or Carl wanted to hear. The hog trough was a shameful and embarrassing place to be kept prisoner. It was located in the pigpen and consisted of two twelve-foot galvanized steel water troughs. The troughs were filled with water and were considerably heavy. The prisoners were tied at the wrists to galvanized steel pieces located within the trough. The ground around the hogs' drinking source was sloppy with mud. Essentially, the prisoners were on their knees with their hands in the water, wrists tied together, and they could go nowhere due to the overwhelming weight of the galvanized steel filled with water. The curiosity of the hogs didn't help much either. They would surround the prisoners and bite at them and lap up the water.

For Marcus, he knew he was at the end of the line. Carl had something else in mind.

"Wait!" Carl yelled. "I have more to add."

Marcus had a deep gut-wrenching feeling that Carl was about to tell the truth. He wasn't going to allow it.

Marcus grabbed Carl by the pack on his back and threw him to the ground before anybody could react. Marcus didn't have to think about a way to kill Carl in a hurry. Years of training and rehearsing these kinds of moments over and over in his mind kept him prepared for the eventuality. It was natural for Marcus to go straight for the throat. He began punching him as hard as he could.

Carl's esophagus collapsed with the first punch. Carl couldn't breathe, but that didn't stop him from fighting back. His body's fight-or-flight response was to release adrenaline. He didn't even know he couldn't breathe.

Marcus punched him as hard as he could five or six times before the guards were able to grab him and pull him from the position of power he had over the suffocating man. It was too late for Carl. The guards beat Marcus as Carl lay on the ground, turning blue. He was trying desperately to breathe, but all Rueben did was watch as Marcus's victim asphyxiated and died.

When Carl was dead and Rueben was done watching the ordeal, he looked over at the guards who were kicking Marcus. He was now on the ground in a fetal position.

"That's enough," Rueben said.

The guards backed away as Marcus vomited on the ground. He didn't care to notice that his face was soaking in his own puke mingled with dirt, giving his bile a brown pasty appearance. He, too, was struggling for air. His diaphragm had been kicked several times, but his injuries were not life threatening. He would recover.

"Now take him to the hog trough," Rueben ordered again. "We'll get some information from him when he's ready to talk."

Two of the guards shouldered their rifles, and each one grabbed Marcus at the elbow. They pulled him over his vomit and headed to the troughs. His head hung down and the tips of his boots dragged against the dry soil. The trip felt like an hour. Within minutes, the guards dropped him at the trough and securely fastened his wrists with rope to a metal bracket that was located within the trough. The guards filled a few five-gallon buckets with well water and dumped them into the watering system.

The hogs came running up as if to fight for the best position for drinking. When they reached Marcus's position, they violently pressed against him. For Marcus, it was reminiscent of a high school mosh pit. The incessant beating he took from the hogs paralleled the beating that he had received at the hands of Rueben's men. There wasn't enough room for all of the hogs at the trough, so there were some biting his arms and legs. He did his best to elbow them off and kick them away. Had he been any more lifeless, they might have eaten him.

After several minutes, the hogs had had their fill. The action died down and the water ran low. The ground beneath him was no longer stable. The mud was slimy and slippery. Marcus's muscles were tired and fatigued. No longer able to support himself, he relaxed himself and the weight of his own body fell prone. He could no longer feel his hands and wrists, which were still secured. The rope had soaked in the water, making it all the tighter and difficult to adjust. The rim of the trough was pressing hard against his forearms, which were now shooting with pain.

Marcus opened his eyes and saw a crowd of people gathering around the pigpen. They were spectators. Each and every one. He was the show that was put on by Rueben as a deterrent to anybody that considered betraying him. Marcus had seen this before, but he assumed he would always be able to meet the strict requirements as set forth by the Enclave. Never in a million years did he believe he would fail a mission or get caught doing something that was unacceptable to Rueben. From the day he joined the Enclave until now, Marcus never considered the possibility that he would be reunited with old friends. With old flames.

Pleasant Bray, Georgia – 10 years earlier

Marcus Guy was nervous. He'd made a promise to his friend Darrick Mitchell that if anything happened to him, he would visit his girl crush, Tonya Ross, and give her a message that he had intended to marry her. It took him a year of routine internet searches to find her.

He wanted to contact her on Facebook, but thought it would be too impersonal and insensitive. When he finally did locate her, he tried to plan out his approach, but nothing seemed feasible. The moment had come, and Marcus was particularly anxious about giving a girl he didn't know bad news.

Well, I'm not going to get anything done just sitting here.

Marcus took a deep breath in and let it out before exiting the car.

Inside the house, Tonya Ross was putting her dishes away. In the background she had the TV on and was listening to a news station, hoping to hear some word on the war and when it would end. Since Darrick's last deployment, she had received two, maybe three letters from him. Then suddenly, they'd stopped coming. It wasn't like him to stop writing letters or coming home from leave to spend time with her. She was dreadfully expecting the worst, but since she wasn't married to Darrick, his unit wouldn't tell her anything.

Knock, knock, knock.

Startled, Tonya dried her hands and headed for the front door. She looked through the peephole and saw a man with flowers. Hoping he was a deliveryman with news about Marcus, she opened the door and smiled at him. The stranger did not smile back, but instead, returned a solemn look of sadness.

"Can I help you?" she asked.

"Are you Tonya Ross?"

"Who's asking?"

"My name's Marcus Guy. I served with Darrick Mitchell in the Marines."

Tonya unlocked the screen door and pushed it open, inviting him into her house. Please, come in. Have a seat," she said, clearing a spot on the couch for him to sit.

He looked about the place and saw several framed pictures of her and Darrick on the bookshelves and on the coffee table. There were no toys or men's work boots to be seen. He was mindful of his environment and trying to absorb as much information as he could about the woman he was preparing to address.

"Um, here, these are for you," he said, handing her the flowers.

"Thank you," she replied, taking them from his hands with a smile. She headed to the kitchen to get a vase to set them in.

Marcus took advantage of her absence and moved closer to the bookshelf. Nestled behind the photos of Darrick were books by Angery American, L. L. Akers, G. Michael Hopf, Boyd Craven, C. A. Rudolph, Tom Abrahams, W. J. Lundy, Franklin Horton, Steven Bird, Patti Glaspy and others. The woman was obviously interested in survival-type books and scenarios. No doubt Darrick had an encouraging effect on her.

"That's me and Darrick when he came home on his first leave," she said, surprising him. She reached in front of him and grabbed a picture. "He doesn't know this, but I put his first letter to me that he wrote from boot camp in the back." She pulled the back of the frame out, and sure enough, there was a tightly folded letter. She held it to her face then put it back. "He's never been a particularly talkative fellow. If he would have wrote more than a page, I wouldn't have been able to hide it there."

Marcus took a step back.

Tonya could read his body language. "You know something, don't you?"

Marcus nodded his head. "It's why I'm here."

Tonya knew the routine. She had seen it on a hundred TV shows – how an officer or somebody important from the military would stop by the house of a KIA and give the bad news. She wouldn't have had that, seeing she wasn't his wife or even a family member. She was thankful to at least hear something. To put her mind at rest. "Tell me what you know."

"The last time I saw Darrick was over a year ago, in Musayib, Iraq. Darrick and I were members of a quick-response force. We were given a snatch-and-grab assignment. It should have been an easy one too, but it turned out to be an ambush. Darrick was a breacher. I was interior perimeter security. Found out later that the bad guys knew who our inside contact was. Instead of killing him, they gave him bad intel. We walked into a trap. Mortars rained from the heavens. RPGs came from everywhere. Security barely made it out alive. Only four members of the security force survived. I was one of them. They told me that nobody on the entry team survived. I didn't finish out my tour with 2nd Marines. I was hospitalized for a couple of weeks and never spoke to anybody from 1st Battalion 2nd Marines again. I was released from active duty after that. When I was ready, I started searching for you. Darrick told me to give you a message."

Tonya was crying.

"He told me to tell you that he had every intention of marrying you."

Tonya began crying even more.

Marcus pulled her in and caressed her. "I don't have the words," he said. He just held her and let her cry on his chest.

Enclave Camp – later that night

"Marcus! Marcus, wake up," a feminine whisper went off in his ear. Marcus startled awake.

Marcus opened his eyes. The crows were circling overhead, and they appeared to be centralized over him. Several had already landed on the hog pen and were watching him, most likely anticipating their next tender morsel. "You shouldn't be here," he said, looking over his shoulder at Kara.

"I'm gonna get you outta here," she said.

"I don't think you understand," Marcus insisted. "You shouldn't be here. It's not safe. Not even in low-light situations."

"It's good. I brought help."

Marcus gave her a dirty look.

"Don't worry," she whispered. "Your secret's safe with me."

"What secret? I didn't tell you anything."

"I'm not stupid. I put two and two together. Besides, you're a sleep-talker. You were rambling on about Tonya in your sleep. It's quite apparent you were dreaming about her."

"Who'd you bring?"

She smirked at him. "Tonya," she said, cutting the rope from his wrists. He was now free to stand up. She grabbed him by the arm and tried to help him up, but his weight was too great for her. "Help me out, bud."

Marcus had a charlie horse in his side from being outstretched for so long. "Where's she at? Someplace safe, I hope."

"I'm here," he heard from the other side of the trough. He looked over to see Tonya standing there.

"Neither of you should be here. I accepted my fate."

"Well, we didn't," Tonya said.

"Then we need to beat some dirt. I doubt you made it in here without being seen."

Tonya threw Marcus's right arm around her neck, and Kara did the same with his left arm. Together they made their way northwest, hoping and praying not to be seen. Tonya and Kara had seen a patrol of three men whom they didn't recognize on their way to rescue Marcus. They agreed to take a slight detour to the north to avoid the men. In so doing, they passed a small one-bedroom house that was dilapidated.

Marcus saw the house on their return and said, "It's getting dark. We need to shelter up."

"We can make it," Kara said. "We're not far now."

"Kara, I can't make it," Marcus said, lying so she'd let him stop at the house. He had no intention of returning to the Mitchells' home.

"Fine. We'll stop, get some rest, and move under cover of darkness."

"No. I'm done for the night. I'll finish in the morning. Those men really did a number on me."

When they reached the house, Kara dropped her pack, and both Marcus and Tonya sat on the floor. It was pitch black and they couldn't see a thing with the roof sheltering them from the moonlight. Within minutes, Marcus was snoring.

"That didn't take long," Kara said. "I figured it would have taken longer seeing how he was recently unconscious."

Tonya didn't answer with the response Kara was expecting.

"Kara, what exactly are you up to?"

"What do you mean?"

"Why are you trying to bring him back home when you can clearly see I lied to keep it from Darrick?"

Kara, being one to discourage dishonesty, chose to answer with a question of her own. "What are you keeping from Darrick that's so important we can risk our lives to save Marcus, but not to bring him home?"

"I can't believe I'm telling you this. Me and Darrick were an item several years ago. We were high school sweethearts. He left his home at an early age, and his dad never bothered to come look for him. My parents took him in under one condition. They saw that he was a troubled teen, so they told him that they would not allow me to date him unless he joined the military. He did. A little before he got out, he joined a special team."

"Magtaf," Kara interrupted.

"Magtaf?"

"The special unit he joined."

"How do you know that?"

"He shared it with me."

"Funny. He never shares that stuff with anybody."

"I'm not anybody."

"Anyway, he went missing. He disappeared for nearly a year. I never heard back from him until –"

"Until what?"

Pleasant Bray, Georgia – 9 years 9 months earlier
Knock, knock, knock.

Tonya jumped up from the couch and ran for the door. She pulled it open and saw Marcus. She reached out and grabbed him, pulling him into the house. "I can't believe you're still knocking," she said, laying a kiss on his lips.

"I wouldn't want to make a beautiful girl like you mad because I'm too rude to knock first," he answered with a smile on his face.

Tonya didn't answer at first. She looked deep into his eyes and gently smiled back at him. Marcus understood. He picked her up and carried her to the bedroom.

Several minutes later, Tonya and Marcus were cuddling under the sheets in the bedroom. Marcus was on his back and Tonya's head was resting on his pectoral muscle. His arm was around her when somebody knocked on the door.

"Expecting company?" Marcus asked.

"No."

Tonya jumped up and ran to the front room, where she peeked through the peephole of the door. Her heart leapt within her.

It's Darrick. Oh God, it's Darrick.

Tonya ran back to the bedroom and picked Marcus's clothes up off the floor and threw them on his chest.

"What's going on?" he asked.

"It's Darrick," she replied with an intensity he'd never heard from her before.

"Darrick?"

"He's alive. He's here. He's on the front porch."

"It can't be Darrick. Are you sure?"

"I'm positive."

Knock, knock, knock, they heard again.

Marcus ran to the front room and looked through the peephole. Astonished, he said, "It is Darrick!"

Tonya pushed Marcus all the way through the house to the back door. "I'm sorry," she said. "I thought he was dead. You told me he was dead. How could you?"

"I –"

Tonya shoved him out before he could finish, and locked the back door. She ran back through the house and pulled the front door open, grabbing Darrick by the arms and pulling him in.

The dilapidated house

"It all makes sense now," Kara said. "Darrick doesn't know that you had an affair with his Marine buddy."

"No, he doesn't, and he can't find out. You're the only other person that knows. That's the reason why we can't take Marcus home."

Kara rested her head against the wall. An inner turmoil within caused her mind to race with thoughts.

Get it out of your head, girl. The man is married. She loves Darrick, but what if Darrick found out about Marcus? Tonya doesn't treat Darrick as good as she ought to. Wouldn't she be happy with Marcus too? I'm alone. I don't know what to do.

Her mind ran wild with questions, and she tried to justify her logic that both of them could be happy if Darrick were to find out. She hadn't yet convinced herself one way or another before she dozed off to sleep.

August 16th

The sun seemed to rise early on the old dilapidated house. Tonya's eyes eased open to let the light in. The ceiling was in shambles and looked as if it would cave in on them at any time. The doors were off the hinges and leaning against the framed corridor. The smell hadn't changed. It was still a pungent mixture of musty construction material and urine. She sat up from her sleeping position and looked over to Kara and Marcus. Kara was still zonked, but Marcus was nowhere to be seen.

Tonya jumped up from the floor and ran outside to see if she could find Marcus. She yelled, "Marcus?"

That startled Kara awake. She jumped up and walked outside with squinted eyes. "What's going on?"

"Marcus isn't here. He must've left sometime in the night."

"Well, that's what you wanted, wasn't it? Marcus saved, but out of the picture."

"Kara, don't start with me."

"I'm just stating the facts. You want Marcus on a string in case something happens to Darrick."

"What gave you that notion?"

"You still have feelings for Marcus, but you're married to Darrick and have a kid with…" Kara interrupted herself. "Oh my god! Andy! You don't even know if Andy belongs to Darrick. If he finds out –"

Tonya went back into the house to collect her gear. She was trying desperately to ignore Kara. Some of what she was saying sounded like psychobabble. The rest sounded accurate. Since Kara knew so much about her and Marcus, Tonya thought it would be best if she played nice with Kara. The last thing she needed was for Kara to let her secret out. She had no idea Kara had been a counselor before the Pulse and had a talent for keeping things quiet. The risk was too great, so she offered her an olive branch. "Kara, I'm really not interested in having a relationship with Marcus. I can't deny that I have feelings for Marcus, but I'm in love with Darrick. He's my husband and the father of my son. I'm asking you, please keep the things you learned here to yourself?"

"Okay," Kara said. She knew about Tonya's cancer. She wasn't going to bring it up, although she was tempted to let Tonya know that she had it in her to wait her out. The thought made Kara feel dirty. She pushed it from her mind, hoping to keep the peace. Despite the way it made her feel, she gave in to the temptation to be patient and to keep Darrick close. She knew that one day Tonya wouldn't be able to be there for Darrick, but Kara would be there to support him. It was the thought of being with Darrick that drove her to stick around. It was the same thought that made her feel terrible and nauseous. She was her own worst enemy.

Kara was so engaged with internal dialogues and conversing with Tonya that she failed to take notice they had been walking for some time, headed back home to the Mitchell house. "I forgot my gear," Kara said, breaking away from Tonya and running back.

Tonya rolled her eyes and kept going. She hadn't liked Kara from the get-go. Attractive, intelligent, seductive – basically everything alluring. Tonya was content walking home alone. She believed that Kara had come and got her to help with Marcus for one reason – to reunite her with Marcus so Kara could have Darrick.

Why didn't she fetch Darrick? Was it because she didn't want to place him in danger? Was it because she assumed there would be no private romance between me and Marcus if Darrick knew? I think she wanted to divide and conquer. There's no doubt in my mind, she wants Darrick to be hers.

***

Kara walked into the dilapidated house to grab her gear.

"I knew I heard a woman's voice," a man said from behind her. It was a grizzled-looking man in a plaid-colored shirt. The sleeves were ripped off and he had a rope in his hand that he dropped when she saw him, and a sniper rifle in the other. He set that down in the inside corner of the doorway.

The encounter startled Kara. When she realized what was happening, she dropped her gear and attempted to yell. Before she could complete a couple of syllables or shift her rifle from her back to her front, the man jumped on her. Kara began hammer punching the man in the chest, but it seemed to have no effect. She was overpowered and weighed half as much as her attacker. Her rifle was swaying about and creating more of a concern than a security device. He knocked her down and took a straddled position over her to maintain his control and eventually was able to grab both of her arms.

Once he had complete control, he wrestled the rifle from her body and slid it away from them. It came to rest at the door. He used the rope that he'd dropped to tie her hands together. The man was clearly in control. Kara was having traumatic memories that she was not able to isolate so that she could focus her attention. The man's intentions were clear. She had seen that look in a man's eyes before. She was terrified.

Once he had her secured, he began going through her belongings. "You have some good equipment here. Both beautiful and prepared." His hands were busy shuffling through the pack while she tried to wriggle her hands free from a poorly secured knot. She knew if she was going to be able to make any kind of an escape, she'd have to do it while he was distracted.

The man began pulling items out of the bag. "A compass, a first-aid kit! That'll come in handy. Rope! Look what I found. Rope!" he said, looking at her. Her beauty caught his attention. He took the rope and started to tie her ankles together, but she kicked him in the chest, knocking him from his position. Kara saw movement at the window behind him. It was Tonya.

She must've heard my yell.

Kara looked at her as the man once again overpowered her and got back into position. Tonya held her finger up to her mouth, signaling that she wanted Kara to remain silent.

Is she going to help me? She's just standing there watching.

The man slapped Kara. She was caught off guard by the sudden jolt to her head and face. She looked back up at the window, and Tonya wasn't there.

She must be sneaking up on him from behind. I'll relax and wait for her to do her thing.

Kara looked toward the door, but she seemed to be alone. The knot that she was working on was finally loosened enough to break free. She punched the man in the neck hard enough to jar his balance. She arched her back just enough to throw him off. She reached into her pocket and pulled out a pocketknife. The man stood up behind her, and she ran out the door, stepping over the rifle as she went. It would have been too risky to grab. He was too close behind. She made a calculated choice to run instead of taking a couple of seconds to grab the rifle and shoot the man.

When she was outside, she looked around, hoping to see Tonya, but she was nowhere. She ran around the side of the house in a futile attempt to find her. Nothing. She turned around to run in the other direction and, in so doing, ran right into her attacker. He winced. She stepped away. Her knife was stuck in his abdomen and it was hanging loosely. "That'll cost you," he said, pulling the knife from his belly.

Mitchell Homestead

Darrick was on the rooftop with his binoculars, hoping to catch a glimpse of Tonya and Kara. He took his rifle with him just in case there was any sign of trouble. The night before, his wife and Kara had run off together and never said a word to anybody, not even Carissa. Darrick had no idea where they went.

Crack.

Carissa and Andy heard the noise from inside the house. Elder Mitchell was unfazed by the morning ruckus. The sound was distinctly rifle in origin.

"Andy, come on, honey, let's go to the safe spot."

Andy jumped up and ran upstairs. Carissa looked out the window and saw Darrick climbing down off the old television antenna with rifle in hand. She stepped outside and said, "Darrick, is everything fine?"

"I don't know. Can you stay with Andy? I just shot somebody."

Carissa pushed the door shut.

Darrick ran down the driveway to find the man he'd shot lying on his side. He was still alive, but bleeding profusely. Darrick kept his rifle pointed at the man just in case he made any sudden movements. He appeared to be unarmed. Darrick let out a sigh of disappointment. He'd shot an unarmed man. He had a holster on his side, but it was empty, as were his hands. Darrick used his foot to roll the stranger over onto his back. He looked to be in his mid-fifties.

"Why are you here, mister?" Darrick asked.

The man didn't answer. Instead, his arms went limp and fell to the ground. With that, Darrick knew he killed him.

"I had to," Darrick said. "He could have been armed. He could have had ill intentions and I wouldn't have known until it was too late." Darrick was alone with the dead man, but spoke aloud as if to reason within himself and to the man he killed that you couldn't walk onto a stranger's property in dangerous times and not expect to get shot.

He felt a hand on his shoulder. He looked. It was Carissa.

"You didn't know. He could've been here for the wrong reasons," she said. Her comment made him feel better, but it didn't answer the burning question on his mind – "Where's Tonya and Kara?"

No sooner than he said those words, he heard the squeaky spring of the back door as it was being opened.

Darrick and Carissa looked at each other, wondering who might be opening it. They both took off running toward the house. Carissa entered the front door, grabbing her rifle and hiding around the corner from the kitchen door. Darrick didn't go in, but instead, brought his rifle up to his cheek and walked a wide angle around the outside of the house. He was fully prepared to shoot another intruder, but when the back door was in his sights, he saw that it wasn't an intruder at all. It was Tonya, and she was alone.

Darrick lowered his rifle. "Where's Kara?"

"That's it? I've been gone overnight and the first question out of your mouth is *where's Kara*?"

"Where've you been?"

Tonya had piped off at the mouth so soon that she didn't consider the various outcomes that might arise from the argument. "I don't have time for this," she answered, hoping to buy some time to think things through.

Darrick ran up to her and grabbed her by the arms. "Where's Kara?" he asked one final time, sensing that something terrible had happened to her. Carissa heard Tonya's voice and knew that she had made it back. Instead of opening the door to let them in, she began to eavesdrop.

"I don't know. She took me to the Omen camp, and we lost track of each other on the way back."

"Why did you go to the Omen camp?"

Tonya shied away from the question.

He asked again, only changing the question a bit. "Where's the Omen camp?"

Tonya refused to answer.

"Tonya, what's going on? What are you hiding from me?"

Carissa burst from the kitchen through the back door. "Tonya's been acting funny ever since some man named Marcus stopped by."

Tonya turned to confront Carissa. The stare was intense.

"Tonya?" Darrick said, pulling her back to face him. "Marcus? Who's Marcus?"

"Marcus Guy," she said, releasing her secret along with her anxiety.

"Marcus Guy from the Marines? He was here? When?"

Carissa butted in. "He stopped in here yesterday when you were out cold on the back table. He's the one who shot the man you just buried. It wasn't Tonya. She took credit for the kill because she's hiding something that she doesn't want you to know. She's refusing to tell anyone. The only other witness to this was Kara, but Tonya seems to have come home without her."

Darrick released Tonya's arm. "Why wouldn't you tell me that Marcus was here? Where is he now?"

Tonya was feeling cornered. She shrugged her shoulders and threw out the first thing that came to her mind. "I don't know. He probably ran off with Kara."

"I don't have time for this right now. There's a dead man in our driveway and I've got to get him in the ground."

"What did I miss?" Tonya asked.

"If you would have been here with me and Carissa, you would have been a part of what was going on."

Tonya gave another dirty look to Carissa.

"Don't you be blaming me for your follies, Tonya. You're the one who disappeared on us in the night. Darrick was being a good husband and watching for you from the roof with his rifle. He saw a trespasser and shot him dead. Anybody who trespasses on this land will be turned to dust."

Tonya felt rage toward Carissa for telling her secret. Compounded with that was the issue at hand; she felt that Carissa was undermining her in front of her own husband. A jealous streak that had reared its ugly head with Kara was now rising against Carissa.

"You know what? The blame is on me," Tonya said with a cynical tone. "A female stranger is welcomed into our home with loving arms, and that's fine, but when a man gets shot, that's on me. Well, halleluiah, I've seen the light," she said, taking off her backpack and throwing it at Darrick.

He caught the pack as she stormed upstairs, presumably to be with Andy, who was still hiding.

Darrick placed the pack on the ground. "I've got another man to plant," he said before leaving.

Carissa secured the back door.

Upstairs, Tonya was entering elder Mitchell's room. "I'm hungry. When's supper?" he yelled at her. She looked at the bowl on the stand and saw that Carissa had been caring for him over the last day. They usually shift swapped, even though Carissa couldn't get him to do anything. "I'll get you something," she said.

"Wait a minute, hon," he interrupted.

She stopped and looked back at him.

"Has Pudge come home yet?"

"Yes. He's home, but he's outside."

"Have 'im break me off a good-sized switch and bring it to me. He's earned another lesson in timeliness."

The words broke Tonya's heart. She'd been too hard on Darrick and realized that she needed to tell him the truth. She was about to concede to the idea when she considered the ramifications of Darrick knowing that Andy might be Marcus's son.

Why couldn't I have waited for Darrick?

An excruciating pain suddenly gripped Tonya's abdominal area.

"Argh," she yelled, grabbing herself. A second pain shot through her. "Argh." She winced. Her diagnosis of ovarian cancer had come on Andy's eighth birthday. She'd thought the painful sexual intercourse she was previously experiencing was a side effect of the difficult labor she'd had with Andy. Later she found out the pain was a symptom of a disease. For the past two years it had gone untreated. She'd felt these pains before, but not usually this intense. In times past, they were tolerable. This time they almost brought her to her knees.

It must be the stress, she thought. *Telling Darrick the truth would only serve to make things worse.*

THE RED CIRCLE

7 The Glade

Darrick patted the loose earth with the back of his shovel to compress the top layer of Oliver Hecht's grave. Now that he was done burying the trespasser, his mind was free to roam. He looked over at Jimmie's grave and again at the graves of Russell and Max, the men who had been killed in his home.

There's more out there, and they're not going to stop coming. Darrick looked around at all the bald spots in the middle of the glade and pondered how many more holes he could dig before running out of room.

I'm going to bury every last one of them, so let's find out how many I can plant.

With that thought, he thrust his shovel back into the earth and dug for the rest of the day and well into the night.

***

August 17th

The next morning came quick for Darrick. Asleep with shovel in hand, "Hey," he heard with a gentle nudge to his ribs. Darrick opened his eyes, blinded by the morning sun. He'd caught about two and half hours of sleep. Hardly enough rest for the day he had planned. Carissa was standing over him. "Hey, big guy. Rise 'n shine."

"What time is it?"

Darrick would normally hold his hand open-palmed and facing him, with his pinky touching the horizon, to determine what time of day it was. He would stack his hands from pinky to index finger and count each finger as fifteen minutes. It was just an estimate because he didn't know the exact time of sunrise. With all the trees in place, he couldn't see the sun, so it was a question he couldn't figure out for himself.

"It's about 6:30," she said.

Darrick stood up. His back was stiff and sore from lying on the flat ground overnight.

"What's with all the plots?" she asked.

"I aim to bury me some more people."

"Are you going to start a fight?"

"Am I going to start a fight? Are you serious? These people killed my brother. They came into our home and threatened to kill us. They captured, tortured, and raped Kara."

"I know, Darrick. You don't have to keep reminding me about Jimmie. He was my husband. Remember?"

"I remember. I just realized last night that we're only buying time. Eventually they're coming for us. All of them against all of us. And believe me, the odds are not looking favorable for us. If we sit here and wait for them, we're as good as dead."

"Well, what's the plan?"

"As you know all too well, I'm a man of action. The way I figure it is to take the fight to them. I aim to capture me a scout and interrogate him for intel. I can find the exact location of the Omen camp and take them out one by one."

"That's not going to work," he heard Tonya's voice saying from the trees.

Both he and Carissa turned and looked to see Tonya walking toward them.

"Why not?" Darrick asked.

"There's too many of them. I was there. I know where they're at and, although I don't know their exact number, I know there's too many for you to take out on your own."

"I don't know if I can trust anything you have to say," Darrick said. It was a risky statement to say to his wife, but after recent events, he felt it was justified.

Tonya looked at Carissa and said, "Can I have a moment alone with my husband?"

Carissa looked to Darrick for approval.

"Go ahead," he said. "We'll be fine."

Carissa gave Tonya a look of distrust that only Tonya could have seen as she walked out of the glade. Tonya felt that she wanted to give her a look back, but recent deep introspection had led her to understand that life was too short to be petty. She knew she was on borrowed time, and because of that, she decided to go ahead and bite the bullet.

"I'm sorry," she said, leading the conversation.

"Sorry for what?" he asked, as if wanting her to admit to some shortcoming or fallacy.

"I've not been honest with you." She sat down next to him and hung her legs over the edge of the grave plot. "You've been hard at work, I see."

"Killing is a full-time job," he answered.

"So you're aiming to kill them all and bury them on your dad's land?"

"As many as I can fit, yes."

Tonya looked around at the morning sky. It was like a prelude to the bombshell she was about to drop. "You know that year you didn't call, write, or email me when you were in Iraq?"

"Yeah."

"It was the longest year of my life. I waited and waited to hear from you. I turned on the six o'clock news and hoped every day that I wouldn't hear that your unit was ambushed or some crazy thing. Do you know that the news doesn't cover what the units are doing?"

Darrick nodded his head in the affirmative. "It's a good thing to leave the media out of war. When they're embedded with us, it compromises the mission." Darrick had never told her about the mission that went bad. She knew he went through a lot, but she'd never heard the story.

"I received a visit one day. Somebody knocked on my door, and when I opened it, it was Marcus."

Darrick's attention was caught. She looked into his eyes and felt awful that she was about to be so brutally honest. "He came to give me the message you asked him to give me. We developed a relationship."

Darrick stood up. "What?"

"We connected on an intimate level, Darrick."

"Are you telling me that you fell in love with Marcus while I was away?"

"He was in the house the day you knocked on the door. I could hardly believe it was you. When I found out you were alive, I made him leave. You're the one I love, Darrick. It was never him. But he was there when you weren't. It wasn't love."

Darrick had both hands on his head. He was pacing around the edge of the grave plots. "Andy was conceived the day I came home," he added, with tears welling in his eyes.

"I don't know," she said.

"Oh God."

"I'm sorry, but I wanted you to know the truth."

"Tell me the rest," he said.

"When you were unconscious on the back table, he saved us from Russell. He was one of the three who came scouting from that Omen group. Apparently, Kara followed him, and he was caught and in the process of being judged for his offenses against them. She came back to solicit my help, and I assisted, eventually aiding in his escape."

"Where is he now?"

"I don't know. He left in the night."

"And where is Kara?"

Tonya didn't answer.

He asked again, "Where is Kara?"

"She didn't make it," she answered reluctantly.

"What do you mean *she didn't make it?*"

Tonya was silent.

Again, he probed. "What do you mean *she didn't make it?*"

"She was killed by some man," she answered with ongoing reluctance.

Filled with rage and indignation, Darrick left the glade and headed straight for the house. He had no intention of forgiving or sparing the lives of any person associated with the Omen.

Tonya followed him out. "Darrick?"

Darrick didn't respond.

"Darrick, I'm talking to you."

At the second more assertive call, he stopped and turned around to confront her. "Oh, now you want to talk to me?"

"Don't be like this."

"Don't be like what? Presumptuous?"

Tonya was speechless.

"Tonya, if you have anything extra you'd like to share, please do it now. Because you're not exactly building a record of trust between the two of us."

Tonya considered sharing with him what had happened at the dilapidated house, but she knew it would only complicate matters, so she remained silent.

"I didn't think so," he said, walking off. Her lack of responsiveness spoke volumes. He thought as he walked then stopped again to confront her. "If you know what happened to her, then why weren't you killed or injured in some way?"

"You'd like that, wouldn't you?"

"There you go again. The art of avoidance. Ignore it and it'll go away." Darrick turned and headed back toward the house. This time he was done arguing. He was convinced that she knew something more about Kara's death, but was keeping it secret. The only rational explanation for Darrick was that she was somehow complicit in her death.

Otherwise, what's there to hide? he thought.

When Darrick and Tonya reached the edge of the wood line, Carissa was there waiting. Tonya could sense that Carissa wasn't so much waiting for her as she was for Darrick. It was nothing she could prove; she was, after all, family, but she was already tired of defending herself against other women who appeared to be interested in her husband, whether real or imagined. Tonya wanted to confront Carissa, but she held her peace. Darrick was her focus, but in the back of her mind, she was worried about Marcus and cared for his overall health and well-being.

Carissa didn't jump in next to Darrick like Tonya imagined she was going to. Instead, she waited for both of them to pass and she followed in line. As she followed Darrick and Tonya, she stopped and took a good look at the old car parked on the edge of the property. "Darrick," she said. Carissa didn't see it, but Tonya rolled her eyes and turned around when he did.

"What's up?" he asked.

"How's your mechanic skills?"

"I took auto shop in high school. What are you thinking?"

"What's the probability of getting that thing running again and just leaving?"

"Leaving? Leave our home, our land, our heritage. Basically, everything we believe in and are willing to die for?"

"What about a contingency?"

"As in, *what if I can't pull it off? What if I can't stop the Omen?*"

"Yes. We have to have a plan B. We can't just assume that everything's going to work out as planned; that everything's going to go the way you think."

"I don't know..."

"Look at it this way – we didn't expect Jimmie to lose his life. We didn't know Kara was going to disappear. We didn't know strangers would be showing up on our land with ill intentions. All I'm saying is there's a lot of what-ifs out there, and things happen that we're not expecting. Let's get the car ready and at least be ready to roll."

Darrick considered her proposal. "I'll take a look at it after breakfast. I'm half starved."

Enclave Camp

Within moments of walking outside, Rueben called out, "Red Circle!" It didn't take long for every fighting-age male to surround him. With pistol in hand, he asserted himself as the man in charge as he inquired into the disappearance of Marcus Guy.

"So nobody's going to take credit for Mark's absence?"

Caw, caw, the crows rang out, breaking the silence. The men on the ground had nothing to say. They each knew what was coming. Answering only meant an expedient death. Not answering bought some time.

Rueben looked around at the crowd. There must've been a couple of hundred men standing in the circle. Each of them happy to live under a heavy yoke if it meant having full bellies, which they did. "Very well," he said, tightening his grip on the pistol. "Rev," he called out.

"I'm here," Cornelius said, stepping through the crowd and joining Rueben at his side.

"Go tell Denver that we have an incompetence issue in our ranks. Ask him how we should deal with it."

"Sir?" Cornelius asked, confused about the request.

Rueben turned to face him. "Did I say something that was confusing to you?"

"No, sir," Cornelius answered, knowing irrefutably that Rueben hated his guts.

Click, Rueben's pistol sounded just as he brought it up to put it in Cornelius's face. "Do it," Rueben commanded.

Cornelius ran off, not knowing where to look for Denver.

"Rev," he said, catching Cornelius's attention.

Cornelius turned around to look at Rueben.

"The ranch house."

Cornelius ran off toward the ranch house. Once there, he turned around to make sure nobody was watching him. The coast was clear. He hated it when Rueben sent him to speak with Denver. However, it was Denver's decisions that gave Rueben power over every member of the Enclave. In doing so, Cornelius was also empowered. He lingered just inside the house for a few minutes before returning to Rueben.

"What did he say, Rev?" Rueben asked Cornelius.

"He said, 'Make an example of them. Show them what accompanies failure,'" Cornelius answered.

Rueben smirked at Cornelius and turned to face the accused. Denver's answer was satisfying. Rueben had an iron fist, but he could not act without authorization from Denver.

"Where's the night watch commander?" Rueben sounded off.

"Here!" a man said, stepping into the inner circle with him.

Rueben took one look at the man and pulled his handkerchief out to cover his nose. "Cody, I expected more from you," he said with a soft voice. It was a personal conversation between the two men. The handkerchief was a problem for Cody and a holy relic of sorts for Rueben. Rueben had a fixed delusion that weakness was contagious. Every time he was near a person he saw as weak, incompetent, disloyal, etc., he would pull his hanky out and cover his nose and mouth with it. In Rueben's mind, this act saved him from catching what he called *the poison*.

Cody knew Rueben held the leadership accountable for their mistakes. It was this fact that scared him. He had no rebuttal to give in his own defense.

Rueben circled Cody with his pistol in hand. Every ear was open to what Rueben had to say. "Everyone here knows that Denver does not tolerate incompetence." The handkerchief was tightly covering his nose and mouth, but his voice was raised loud enough to carry his message to every listener who had an ear to hear with. Even if they didn't, it wasn't his words that spread the message he wanted them to receive. It was his actions.

The crowd stood silently and watched to see what Rueben would do next. When he made his third circle around Cody, he stopped behind him and raised his pistol to the back of his head. He pulled the trigger, letting loose an explosion of energy from the tip of his firearm. The men standing to the front of Cody were instantly covered in red droplets of blood and brain matter. Cody's body fell to the ground.

"Feed him to the hogs," Rueben said, handing his pistol to Cornelius.

Cornelius reached into his pocket and pulled out a replacement bullet. He ejected the magazine and inserted the round. It was a manner of control for Rueben. Everybody saw it, so they knew who was in charge. Cornelius returned Rueben's pistol about the time two men were dragging Cody's body out of the Red Circle gathering.

"That was merciful," Rueben sounded off, pointing to Cody's lifeless body as it went. "I don't have to show you mercy. Each of you has a belly full of food and water. The world outside the Enclave is burning. The masses are starving. The fruits of my success are shared with you, and you eat good because of it; but when you fail, I fail – and when I fail, then the fruits of my failure are also shared with you. Each of you made an agreement when I saved you from certain death. Each of you chose to follow me, and the prerequisites were minimal. These are the terms of our agreement. Let me remind each of you that you all solemnly swore within the Red Circle to be one with the Enclave. Blood in, blood out."

Before dismissing the men, Rueben looked around at the Red Circle and added one final remark. "Whoever was on night watch at the time of Marcus's escape, to you I say this – your failure was paid in full by the spilling of Cody's blood. Do not fail again. Sin requires a sacrifice – let's tighten things up. A new night watch commander will be appointed this evening. I expect better next time. This Red Circle gathering is concluded."

The men left the circle, parting ways. Rueben, his three guards, and Cornelius remained. Looking about to make sure there were no other persons present, Rueben said, "Has either of the two trackers reported back with any findings?"

"Not yet. I set him out to keep watch just like you commanded. It was smart to believe that something was amiss. They came for him, just like you said they would. My guess is that soon we'll be hearing back from him that he's located the people responsible for five missing men and how Marcus is connected to them."

"Good. For your sake, you'd better pray for a positive outcome."

The one-liner was a calm and direct threat to Cornelius's life. Rueben made sure that his eyes were connected to Cornelius's when he said it. He pushed past Cornelius and headed toward the ranch house. His three guards followed behind, also pushing by Cornelius.

Cornelius walked to a shady spot over by the barn. There was something about that spot that seemed to draw in the cooler air. It smelled like cattle, but was still better than baking in the sun. Byron was there, too. Seeing Byron with his wife and two children triggered him in some way that made him mad at Rueben. Cornelius looked around. There were too many people to say anything to Byron about the coming cleanse, but the need to express himself after the treatment he'd received from Rueben was irresistible.

"Byron," he said, walking up to him.

"Hey, man. That was crazy, huh?"

"Huh? Oh, you mean the way Cody was killed and dragged off as hog food?"

"Yeah. I'm glad my wife and daughters didn't have to see that."

"Um, about that… I think we need to have a talk about them."

"About my wife and daughters? Why do you say that?"

"Take a look around, Byron."

Byron did just as Cornelius asked. Nothing was out of the ordinary. "What, pray tell, am I looking for?"

Cornelius looked toward the ranch house. He saw no sign of Rueben, so he went back to work on Byron. "Look, I've said and done horrible things, but women and children shouldn't be exposed to any of this."

"I know, right! Thank God the women and children aren't allowed to be a part of the Red Circle gatherings."

"Byron, there are no women and children."

What Byron heard was something he'd noticed several times over, but dismissed as happenstance. "Yeah, why is that?"

"Because they have no part to play in all of this. They're mouths to feed and nothing more. They're kept around when the steaks are plentiful, maybe used as bartering chips when needed, but for the most part –" Cornelius stopped talking when he saw Rueben looking out the window of the master bedroom of the ranch house. "Never mind. I just thought you should know," he said before walking off and leaving Byron alone with no answers.

***

Rueben closed the window curtain and continued his talk with Denver as he watched Cornelius through the translucent curtains. "Cornelius is too shady. I don't trust him."

"What's not to trust? He carries out your every command. You treat him like a dog, and still he comes to you."

"I don't know. There's something suspicious about him. It's like he's talking about me behind my back. Even now, as I address the matter, he seems nervous that I've caught him doing something he ought not be doing."

"You're just being paranoid. Cool your jets and think on the things I've told you. Until he actually betrays us, there's no reason to suspect him. He's a godly man, and you know as well as I do, we need God on our side."

"Where was God when we were being held against our will at Three Springs Maximum Security Forensic Center?"

"Don't raise your voice to me! I know all too well what we went through at that wretched place. He held us together and brought us through. Think back. Remember as I have."

Three Springs Maximum Security Forensic Center
Three Springs, Georgia – Two years earlier
9:00 p.m.
"Reisner," a security guard called out.

Reisner walked out of his room and up to where the guard was standing. There was a nurse at the door, wearing an all-white uniform. He approached her and stood next to another security guard, who was there for her protection.

"It's time for your meds, Reisner," the lady nurse said. Her voice was soft and her eyes were piercing. When he didn't answer, she said, "You are Rueben, aren't you?"

Rueben stood in front of the two staff members while they each confirmed his identity, even though he refused to confirm his own ID. She looked down at her medical record book and saw Rueben Reisner's photograph and his list of medications. She looked up at his face and confirmed it was him. Rueben looked suspiciously at the security guard standing next to her.

"Good morning, Rueben," the guard said, taking a jab at his mentality.

"I told you not to call me that!"

The guard smirked. "Take your pills or you'll regret waking up this morning."

The first security guard heard the second's threat to patient Reisner. "Is there a problem?" he asked, walking up to join the first.

"No, Reisner here thinks he can talk smack. I told him to take his pills. If he doesn't, we'll strap him to the restraint bed and give them through a needle."

"Well, actually, these meds don't come injectable," the nurse said.

"No matter. We will make good on our part," the first security guard said. "Now take 'em."

Rueben looked down at the meds and saw a syringe.

"You'd better leave," the first security guard told the nurse, having seen Rueben eyeballing the syringe. The nurse left, and the two security guards grabbed Rueben. He immediately pulled away from the grasp of the smaller weaker second guard and turned around to punch the guard who was originally next to the nurse. He hit him square in the jaw, but the second guard was already pushing the emergency duress button that each of them were required to wear. Once pushed, the alarm sent a signal to the hospital's central control room that told the staff there was an emergency situation on that security guard's assigned unit.

The second guard grabbed Rueben in a bear hug. The nurse was scrambling to get out the door when the first security guard regained his composure. He grabbed Rueben by the back of the head and forced him down onto the floor. With the other security guard's weight on his back, it wasn't that difficult to get him down. They each started punching Rueben with hammer fists in an attempt to subdue him. He was very strong and easily overpowering the two men. If not for the several other guards who responded to the alarm, he might very well have killed them.

Once the others were on hand, they carried him to a room, where they began strapping him down to a bed. Several guards held his body down while others worked feverishly to secure his ankles. The whole time, Rueben was screaming for Denver and saying, "I can't breathe, I can't breathe," but Denver never came – not until the Pulse. Rueben's wrists were still unsecured when the lights suddenly went out.

"What's going on?" someone yelled. It was pitch black. Blacker than that even. The security room where they worked to restrain Rueben was deep within the mental facility. There were no windows, only doors that led to other rooms with no windows. It was a deep, heavy, smothering darkness.

"He's got my –" one person started to say, then was suddenly silenced.

There was a gurgling sound.

"Argh," another person screamed.

"What's going on? What's happening?" various staff were heard yelling. Several more screams, yells for help, and wincing sounds were made by staff.

"Let's get out of here," Rueben heard Denver's voice saying in the darkness. "Your legs are loose. Never mind the staff. They're weak, but we're strong."

"I can't see a thing," Rueben said to Denver in the darkness.

"We're going to have to feel our way through the darkness to the light. Remember this moment, Rueben. There will be times in your life when you think you have no light to guide you, but if you look deep enough, in the right spots, you'll see your way out." Denver was the smart one who would speak simple and encouraging words to live by. Rueben ate it up. He respected Denver's intelligence, strength, and patience. "Mind your step so that you don't trip over the staff," Denver said.

It wasn't the staff Rueben was tripping on, but it was their warm blood on the newly waxed floors. It was slippery and Rueben needed to maintain three points of contact as he maneuvered through the area.

Bodies lined the walls of the room as he made his way through the door that the staff had left open as they came running in to assist.

There wasn't a ton of staff at Three Springs, but when they spoke, he recognized the voice and avoided them. Every once in a while, he would feel that he was alone, so he'd call out to Denver, "Denver, are you here?"

"Of course I'm here. Stay on task. Head for the exit."

As Rueben made his way through the halls, the darkness became less and less prevalent. Light from the front door began to saturate the facility's corridors. When he was able to see, he looked around, but couldn't find Denver. Seeing several employees of the facility congregating near the exit, he worried that he might be detected. They were standing in groups, talking about the power outage and other weird things that had happened the moment the lights went out. None of their cell phones were working. Even their cars would not start. Everything that had a circuit board, every single electronic device, including digital watches and battery-operated clocks and devices, stopped working at the same time.

"I heard about this. China, Korea, Russia, the UK and the US were all arguing about electromagnetic pulse weapons on the news last night. I figured it would never happen; now it seems that I was wrong."

Rueben began to panic. He looked around again, not seeing Denver. He held his shirt up over his face to cover his nose and mouth, paranoid that he might breathe in the deadly poison. He walked right on out the door like that. Nobody questioned him. Nobody stopped him. He was free.

Rueben joined the crowd of people who were walking up the highway. There were several cars parked along the way, but none of them were working. Occasionally, he would see an older model vehicle driving down the road.

Eventually, Rueben reached a gas station. Standing in the doorway was an employee of the facility. "I'm sorry, we're closed," he said, forbidding him access.

"I just need to use your restroom."

"I'm sorry, but the manager gave me explicit orders not to let anybody in until the power comes back on."

Rueben looked around. When he was content that there were no witnesses, he grabbed the man by the throat and pushed him into the store. There was a struggle, but Rueben's hands were tightly in place as he choked the man to death from the low-mounted position. Rueben held his breath for the entire duration of the struggle, taking only small gasps of air to survive. He was fearful that the man's weakness would transfer to him through his breath. The deadly poison surrounded his victim. He was oozing with it. Once the man was lifeless, Rueben stood up and let out a powerful exhale and gasped for his own air. He grabbed a handkerchief from a sell stand and used it to cover his nose and mouth. He entered the bathroom, where he looked in the mirror.

"Well done," the man in the mirror told him. "I told you to stay on task, and you stayed on task. I told you to feel your way through the darkness, and you felt your way to freedom. Now look at you shine. You and I can be a beacon of light for all who are lost in darkness, but only in due time. Look around you."

Rueben ran outside to look at all the weak people walking down the street. Men, women, children – all weak. He ran back to the bathroom, where the man in the mirror continued to speak to him. "There's too many, Rueben. Too many to care for; too many to feed. In time, their numbers will dwindle. There's going to be a die-off and, like sheep that can't survive without their shepherd, they will fall prey to men like you. Together we can make logic out of the mayhem."

Enclave Camp – Two years later
"I remember," Rueben said, turning to face his dual personality, Denver, in the mirror.

"I never gave you a reason to trust me, but you have. Trust Cornelius until he gives you a reason not to."

"You're probably right," Rueben said, turning back to look through the window at Cornelius. "I need a reason not to trust him," he whispered. His intention was sure – betray Denver by killing Cornelius. But how? Denver always knew what Rueben was up to. It would prove to be a difficult thing for Rueben to get away with secretly betraying him. Cornelius was up to something. Rueben could sense it and was confident of that. Denver would never question Rueben's judgment if the evidence was credible.

I'll set the trap, and when the Rev takes the bait, I'll know he's a traitor, he thought.

Mitchell Homestead

"So when are you going to look at the car?" Carissa asked Darrick.

His mouth was full of eggs when he was asked the question. "I gave it some thought, and I think it would be the safest route for you."

"For me?" she said, looking across the table at Tonya. Darrick was standing against the kitchen sink. The table was too small to seat the whole house. Elder Mitchell was in the front room with a tray over his lap. Tonya, Carissa, and Andy were sitting at the small round table. "What do you mean, *for me*?"

"I'm not going anywhere. If you think it's too dangerous to stay here, then by all means, I'll fix the car and you can leave. I'm staying to defend this place."

Tonya was upset at his answer. "That doesn't even make sense. If the car works, let's leave. Think of Andy's safety. Think of my safety."

Darrick knew they were right. In his heart, he knew the safest move would be to pack up and leave. In his mind, he had another idea – to eradicate the Omen.

Page **139** of 181

"They killed Jimmie. They killed the Berts and tried to kill us. They took Andy hostage and raped and tortured –"

"We're tired of hearing you defend Kara, Darrick," Tonya interrupted. Both Darrick and Carissa gave a sour look to Tonya over her abrupt and insensitive remark.

"What's your problem with Kara?" Darrick asked.

"I saw how she looked at you. She was moving in on you. You're my husband, not hers. You treated her a little better than you treated me, and that didn't sit well with me." Tonya no sooner said that statement than she fell off the chair and onto the floor. "Argh," she cried out. Darrick and Carissa ran to her.

"What's going on, Tonya?" Carissa asked.

"She's been unmedicated for too long. She's in pain. I think it's spreading."

"What's spreading?"

"Jimmie didn't tell you?"

"Tell me what?"

"Tonya has ovarian cancer. It should be in its advanced stages by now, and there's nothing we can do about it."

Overwhelmed by the news, Carissa stood up and backed away from them both.

Darrick saw her response. "Don't worry, it's not contagious."

"No, I know it's not. It's not that – it's just… it's just so much to take in. First James gets sick, then Jimmie dies, now this. There's just so much going on. It's overwhelming."

"Don't count me out yet," Tonya said, trying to get to her feet.

Darrick assisted her and came to a realization that they were going to need a car. "Okay," Darrick said, seemingly changing the subject.

Carissa and Tonya looked at Darrick. "Okay what?" they said almost simultaneously.

"I'll look at the car right away. I'm sorry, Tonya. I've been red with anger, and I've forgotten what matters. Dad's old and feeble;

you're getting sicker every day. If something does happen and we have to flee on foot – there's just no way we can make haste with those factors working against us."

"It's always nice to know you're a burden," Tonya said with a sarcastic tone.

"It's not that."

"I know," she said, touching him on the arm. "I'm just glad you've come to your senses."

Darrick looked at Carissa. "How long has the car been sitting there, and what do you know about its condition?"

"It died right there in front of the house."

"The Pulse killed it?"

"No. It's one of the models that can survive an EMP. It just ran out of gas."

"How long ago?"

"Several weeks after the Pulse, maybe. I don't really remember."

Darrick gave it some thought. "Can you take care of Tonya while I go look at the car, then?"

"I don't need caring for. I'm fine," Tonya said to him.

"Suit yourself. I'm going outside."

Darrick shoveled what was left of his eggs down his throat. "Who woulda thought a woodburning stove could cook so good?" he said on the way out the door.

Carissa looked at Tonya and said, "There's some unresolved issues between us."

"Like what?" Tonya asked, offended by the remark.

"I was hoping you would tell me why you've been shooting me so many dirty looks."

Tonya sighed. "I'm so sick of playing the antagonist in this story. I'm just going through a lot. That's it. I might be a little emotional. There's a lot of changes going on in this body that I can't control."

"I forgive you," Carissa said, smiling at Tonya.

Tonya returned the smile.

***

Darrick used a machete to hack away a large portion of the overgrowth that was hiding the car. The hood was popped and he sat there staring under the hood and thinking out loud. "She's been sitting here for about two years, so the carburetor will probably be nasty. The gas can may be full of condensation, and the starter is likely going to be a problem." He pulled the dipstick out and discovered that there was almost no oil in the car. As he thought about that, he figured the cylinders would also most likely be dry, which could cause a problem even if he was able to get it started. *Impossible*, he thought. *There's no way this thing's gonna run. I can probably get some gas from Dad's old tractor, but it'll be bad from sitting so long. I don't see this working out.*

***

Several yards away, nestled invisibly within the foliage of the Mitchells' environment, Kara sat with a sniper rifle in hand. She was pointing it at the Mitchells' property, surveying the area. Looking through her scope, she saw Darrick hunkered down in the engine of the old Torino. He was in her crosshairs, but her finger was not on the trigger. Darrick wasn't the target. She scanned from right to left back over to the house and looked through the windows of the house. This would have been an impossible task without the high-powered scope, but with this rare item, she was able to see movement in the kitchen area. It was Tonya. Kara placed her finger on the trigger and snugly secured the butt of the rifle against her shoulder. *This is it,* she thought. *Relax. This is what needs to be done. She's a bad person. Evil, really. I can do this.*

Kara's finger began to apply pressure to the trigger. *What am I doing?* Disappointed in herself, whether for lack of courage or lack of internal tumult, she pulled the rifle away from her shoulder and abandoned her mission.

***

Darrick was so frustrated that the task at hand was an impossibility without the necessary resources that he slammed the car's hood down. With the giant blind spot out of the way, he was startled to see Kara standing there near the back of the car with a sniper rifle in hand.

"Kara! Where have you been?"

"Shhh," she said, running around to the front of the car and grabbing him by the arm. She led him to the side of the car that faced away from the house, and knelt down, pulling Darrick down with her.

"You wanna tell me what's going on?" he insisted.

"Where should I start?" she said, looking to the clouds. "Oh yeah, your wife left me to die."

"Left you to die?" Darrick asked, confounded at the statement. "Start at the beginning. That's a bold accusation."

Kara thought about all the ways she could address the situation. She knew so much about Marcus and Tonya and their relationship. What she didn't want to do was to cause Darrick any heartache.

"What do you know about Marcus?"

"Marcus and I were in the Marines together. I already know he was here."

"You do?"

"Yeah. He's in the area, Tonya tried to keep it from me, but Carissa spilled the beans."

Kara was surprised that Darrick already knew. He could read her body language as she turned her head downward and looked at the ground.

"You seem disappointed that I know," he said.

"Not disappointed, just shocked. Did she tell you that while you were recouping, she and I went to the Omen camp and saved Marcus from certain death?"

"She told me that she went to the Omen camp, but refused to tell me why she went. She said she was separated from you, and she wasn't sure where you went. She was being very secretive about most of the events of that night. What do you know?"

"She knew exactly where I was. She watched through a window as I was being assaulted and bound with my own rope by some smelly scumbag. She shushed me then vanished."

"I'm sure there's some explanation."

"Darrick, she saw that I was overpowered, and she left me to die."

Darrick was shocked by the news that Tonya would neglect to help Kara in a life-threatening situation. Kara saw that her story was affecting him. She was conflicted in her heart about how to proceed. She had an interest in Darrick, but he was married – married to a negligent cowardly woman who had left her to die.

She doesn't deserve his protection. If she left me to die, what will she do to him or Andy?

It was her thought about Andy that sparked a fire in her mind to tell him about Marcus and Tonya's moment the day Darrick walked back into her life.

"Darrick, there's more," she said.

He looked at her with sad eyes, hoping she didn't have some devastating new information. He could tell that she was being sincere, and the story she shared about being assaulted and left for dead was believable, just disheartening.

Kara looked into his eyes and knew that what she was about to tell him would destroy his world. The message was on the tip of her tongue, but she couldn't spit it out.

"What is it?" he asked.

She just looked back into his eyes and said, "The Omen is two or three hundred strong. I think we need to cut our losses and vacate the property."

"You sound like Carissa," he answered. "I'm not necessarily proud of being my father's son, but this is my property now. Mine! I'll defend it with my life. It's why I joined the Marines – to defend the things that matter most. To live free and die hard."

"Freedom is an illusion. Even when we had a working government, which we haven't heard from for two years now, we were taxed into oblivion. Nothing's free."

"I'm free! And there's no one going to tell me I can't live here and do what I want on my land."

"None of us will be left alive to live on this land; that's what I'm trying to tell you."

Darrick was becoming frustrated with the argument. The car couldn't be fixed; his dad was too slow to make a trip anywhere; his wife was slowly dying; there just wasn't a plausible answer that ended with the group making it away as a whole. "Where will we go? How will we live?"

"We're racing against the clock. How many men have come here and not returned? It's only a matter of time before they find us. They may already know we're here, and if that's the case, we're all sitting ducks."

Darrick turned to face the east. He knew the Omen was just a few miles away, and everything he knew about them was bad. He tried to rationalize in his mind, but deep down he knew that his promises to bury them all on his land were empty and idle threats. His other idea, to take the fight to them, seemed more viable, but equally ridiculous. At least it would buy time for him and his family to vacate the property and make it out safely.

"Kara, you said you were attacked by a man. Was he one of them?"

"I don't know. I think so. Why?"

"Because they seem to be either paired or in groups of three. That begs the question, *where's the second or even third man?*"

Darrick made up his mind. "Kara, you're stronger than both Carissa and Tonya. You need to lead them to safety, and you need to do it as soon as possible."

"Uh, I don't think your wifey is gonna buy into that deal."

"I'm not going anywhere with her," Tonya said. She was eavesdropping from the front yard and had heard the butt end of their conversation. She walked out from behind the corner of the house to reveal herself. Kara and Darrick had been so preoccupied with their discussion that they'd let their guard down and weren't paying attention to their environment. Even Carissa was listening from the window of the front room.

"Is that why you left me to die back at that old shack?" Kara shouted, stepping out from behind the car.

"You're not welcome here," Tonya answered.

"That's not for you to decide. Darrick is the man of the house, last I saw."

Tonya was done. She stormed toward Kara with her fists tightly clinched and decided that she was going to beat her to death. Darrick jumped between them and faced off against Tonya.

"Are you taking her side?" Tonya asked.

"That depends. Did you leave her alone to die?"

Tonya didn't answer, but her body language gave away everything. Darrick could read her like an open book. Catching on to her deception, he asked again, "If you knew she was being attacked, why did you leave her alone?"

"I was scared," she answered. Her true answer was still a secret that only she knew. She wanted Kara dead for more than one reason. At the time, Kara was the only other person who knew of Marcus's and her relationship. That was later revealed to Darrick, but the other issue was that she knew Andy was conceived on the night of her encounter with both Marcus and Darrick, a clandestine moment in time that she wanted to die with Kara.

Kara was good at detecting deception. The next thing she said blurted out of her mouth without any more forethought or control. "She wanted me dead because of Andy."

Tonya's face turned pink. Darrick heard the words and saw Tonya's reaction. "What do you mean, *because of Andy?*" he asked.

"Marcus was with Tonya the night you came back," Kara announced. "Tonya knew that I knew and wanted me to die so that you'd never find out the truth."

"Tonya?" Darrick said, looking to her for an answer.

The only answer she gave him was a cold shoulder. He returned it in kind by walking away toward the house.

"Where are you going?" Kara asked.

"Away," he answered sharply. "And I hope that by morning, you guys have your drama resolved," he said as he went.

"Darrick, wait," Tonya shouted.

Darrick stopped in his tracks and turned around.

"I thought you were dead."

There was nothing left for Darrick to argue. She'd moved on with his best friend because he wasn't there for her. Marcus was. What was she to do?

"I know," he answered, giving her a hint of hope for forgiveness. "I have some thinking to do." Darrick ran off toward the glade. Tonya and Kara were left standing there alone in awkward silence.

Enclave Camp
"Rev," one of Rueben's guards shouted.

The shout startled Cornelius. "Yes?"

"Ten-Stitches would like to speak with you."

"Okay. Where is he?"

"He's waiting for you by the well."

The area Rueben was calling him to was an older section of property that hadn't been used in years. From the way the place was set up, it appeared that the ranch house was not actually the original location of the house. The owners had left the old foundation intact but demolished the old house. When the new ranch home had been built, a new foundation was poured to meet the specific requirements for the upgrades.

Cornelius was immediately frightened. Rueben had never requested to speak to him in a location so remote. The well was away from the immediate property and concealed behind the oldest barn on the property. It rested a few yards from the outhouse and served no other purpose than that of an antique toilet.

Instead of reporting immediately to Rueben, he went to locate the man who had identified himself as Byron. He seemed like a nice fellow and one whom he could trust information to. Besides, Byron had something to live for, and if this was going to be Cornelius's last day on earth, he needed to clear his conscience first.

"Byron, do you have a minute?"

"Hey, what's up?"

Cornelius saw Byron's wife and daughters were still with him, and that gave him hope that he had time to act. "Listen, I don't have much time, but there's something you need to know."

Byron could see that there was something serious going on. "What is it?"

"You have to get your wife and daughters away from here. Immediately."

His wife and daughters were standing nearby, so they stood up and joined Byron to hear everything he had to say. "And why's that?" he asked.

Cornelius was afraid to say what needed to be said. There was no easy way to say it, so he just said what first came to the forefront of his mind. "Look around, Byron. There's no women or children because Rueben takes them and they're never seen again."

"Takes them? Takes them where?"

"To Denver, Rueben's alter ego, his split personality. However you want to say it. Rueben is Denver, and if your wife and children can't meet the rigorous demands of survival of the fittest, they'll disappear too." When Cornelius was done speaking his truth, he could see the terror in Byron's wife's and daughters' eyes. "I'm sorry you had to hear that, but I'm afraid for my own life, and you should save what you have left of yours."

When he concluded his warning to Byron, he made haste to meet with Rueben over by the old well on the other side of the property.

"I was just about to give up on you, Rev," Rueben said. He was leaning against an old wooden fence when Cornelius made his approach.

"I always come when you call for me."

"Indeed. There's been times I've questioned your loyalty, but I know in the end, you've done whatever was required of you. After all, Denver seems to have a lot of trust in you. Why do you think that is?"

"Because I've been a faithful member of the Enclave. I provide spiritual counseling and advice to Denver. He likes me because I'm steadfast."

Rueben took his weight off the fence and started walking to where Cornelius was standing near the well. When Cornelius saw him coming, he nervously looked around and only saw two of Rueben's three guards. He now had legitimate reasons to fear for his life. His eyes began darting around the horizon, expecting to be shot at any time.

"That look," Rueben said when he was close enough to Cornelius to grab him.

"What look?"

"That look on your face. It's the look that makes me nervous to be near you." Rueben pulled his handkerchief up over his nose and mouth and then took a step back. "You're poisonous," he said with disgust in his voice.

"I'm not poisonous or contagious, Rueben, I assure you."

Cornelius saw Rueben look past him. He turned to look at what Rueben was seeing. His third guard was standing there in the distance, nodding his head.

"What's going on, Rev? I thought you said you were loyal, faithful, and steadfast?"

"I am."

"Come. Walk wit me," Rueben said, stepping out in front of Cornelius.

Cornelius followed a couple of steps behind Rueben, being cautious as he went. The two guards who were with Rueben were following closely behind them. Rueben led him toward the old oak tree on the other side of the ranch house. It was hundreds of years old and reached high into the sky. The lower branches had been trimmed off prior to the Pulse, giving it an extra-long trunk. When they turned the corner of the house, the old tree came into view. Cornelius was terrified by what he saw. Quite possibly the most sadistic and twisted scene of his life. Hanging by their necks, several feet off the ground, were Byron, his wife, and his two young daughters. Their feet were still kicking and their arms were flailing about as they spun from the hangman's nooses. With each movement, the nooses tightened until they each stopped kicking and hung limp. Cornelius's eyes were full of tears, and his mind was full of both sadness and rage.

"I will give you a head start, Rev. When I get back from my meeting with Denver, I am sure he will have authorized your execution. Good luck."

Cornelius took off running as fast as he could. Rueben watched the direction he took off running in and turned himself toward the house. His next move was to visit Denver and get authorization for the order to kill the traitor Cornelius.

REUNION

The Glade
Mitchell Homestead

Darrick was sitting alone in the glade next to his brother, Jimmie's grave. He was contemplating his life and how much had happened in the past few years. His conclusion was that he felt he didn't have a lot left to live for. His dad was senile and didn't know Darrick's face; his wife was slowly being taken by a cancer in her ovaries, and her prognosis wasn't good; his son, Andy, might not even be his son; his brother had been murdered by men who didn't know him; and to top it off, there was a company-sized group of raiders fixing to make their move onto his property at any moment.

His mind had spent some time on these matters, and his gut told him to run, but his logic told him his dad wouldn't make any trip away from the shelter of his home. Tonya would most likely slow them down in time. The only thing he could think of was to lure the group away from the homestead, but even that was only buying a moment. In time, the property would be discovered. If not by the raiders, then by some other group of hostiles.

With his mind made up, he geared himself for a talk with the women. How would he approach them with the news? He knew in his heart they would try to talk him out of it, but they had to go alone. Perhaps to Pontybridge, a town several miles south, but even that might be laden with dangers. At least there, they could take cover and wait for the Omen to move on to another area. There were so many details. So many things to consider that weighed on the decision. Each move affected the other in some way.

"Mitchell," a familiar voice said from behind him. Caught off guard by the silent approach, Darrick didn't have his rifle ready. It was Marcus.

"You don't need that with me," Marcus said, seeing Darrick's tight grip on the rifle. "What are our assets?"

Darrick stood up and walked over to Marcus and punched him square in the face. Marcus took the punch.

"I suppose I deserved that. I just want you to know that we both thought you were dead," Marcus said, rubbing his jaw.

"I was in rehab from wounds sustained in that mortar attack. I was told the official report was that I was MIA until they found my body floating on the bank of the Euphrates. It took months before I could even walk a straight line. I have plates in my left leg, shrap in my chest, and a few really cool scars."

It was the last comment that made Marcus smile. "You haven't changed much, buddy."

"More than I show."

"So, what's our list of assets?"

"Me, you, Tonya, my sister-in-law Carissa, Kara, whom I believe you've already met, several acres of hilly land, some woods and a couple of rifles, pistols, and a handful of ammunition."

"That's not enough."

"I know. I was going to lure them away from the homestead and maybe buy the family a head start. They can hide at Pontybridge until the fight is over or they move on."

"They still don't know where you are."

"How can you be sure?"

"I've been doing some thinking of my own. You're about the only family I have left, Mitchell. Anyway, while I was doing my thinking thing, I saw a tracker on the plains. I only saw him in the distance, so I hunkered down and hid. There should be two, but I never saw the other. We need to be careful. He could be watching us now."

"I might be able to get some information on where the second one is."

"How so?"

"I understand that Tonya and another woman named Kara helped you get away from the Omen?"

"The Enclave."

"Huh?"

"It's called the Enclave. But Denver hates it being called the Omen, so call it that if you want to."

"Okay, well, it's a long and traumatic story, but Kara was captured by a lone man and assaulted by him. Apparently, Tonya left her to her own fate and made off without her. I'm thinking she may know something about the guy."

"Can we go find out without stirring up a hornet's nest?"

"That depends," Darrick said.

"On what?"

"On whether or not you still have feelings for Tonya."

"Darrick, I can't make the past go away, and I can't make old feelings stay down, but you have my word, I would never do anything to cause you grief. What you and Tonya have is legit. I won't interfere."

"One more question…"

"Sure."

"Why did you need saving? What did you do, and how did you come to be with them?"

"That's a lot of questions! I was already in the area when the Pulse hit us. I did like most people did and tried to make do for a while, but when I understood what was really happening, I went into survival mode. You know as well as I do that a man in survival mode is full-on beast mode! I did what I had to do to survive. I stole, killed, and destroyed to feed myself. I did that for some time. When the Enclave came through the area, I took the Red Circle pledge."

"What's that?"

"Basically, I swore my life to the Enclave in exchange for food, shelter, and water. Later, I was added to a group of scouts and directed to find Shawn, Larry, and Maxim. That excursion led me here, where I found you and Tonya. Now that I've betrayed them, they won't rest until I'm dead. I tried to distance myself from you to keep them away from you and Tonya, but the more I thought about it, the more I realized they weren't going to stop until you were dead, too. I figure we're stronger together. So I committed myself to that old brotherhood we shared in the Corps. I've got your six, Mitchell."

"It's good to hear. What do you think we should do?"

"There's a group of survivalists south of here, in Pontybridge. There's people there I know, but they're not doing so well. I'm not sure if they'll take us in, but it's worth a try."

Darrick smiled at Marcus and nodded his head. "Okay. Let's end this."

Later

Tonya, Carissa, and Andy were sitting in the front room. Carissa was reading a book to Andy, and Tonya was curled upright on the couch when the secret door knock was heard on the front door.

Tonya stood from the couch and said, "I'll get it."

She opened the door and saw Darrick. Right behind him was Marcus. She was shocked to see them both together for the first time.

"Where's Kara?" Darrick asked.

"Out back where she belongs."

"Me and Marcus need to have a word with her," he said, pushing past Tonya. They cut through the house to get to her. Marcus could feel the tension. He'd also noticed Tonya's expression when Darrick asked for Kara. He wondered how much trouble his presence brought with it.

Kara was sitting on the wooden table out back when the door opened. She looked over and saw both Darrick and Marcus together.

"Together again." She smiled, sitting up to meet them both.

"Kara, I think you've already met Marcus. Can you tell us what you know about the man who attacked you yesterday?"

She had a clear bruise on the left side of her face where the man had hit her.

"Well, he was wearing a plaid shirt, and the sleeves were torn off –"

"But was he alone?" Darrick interrupted.

"I thought I already established that. Yes, I think he was, but I had no way of knowing for certain. He was the only one at that location, yes."

"I'm sorry I never asked before, but how did you get away?"

"It's alright. I managed to free myself from the rope he used to restrain me. After that I stabbed him in the gut with my knife. He came at me again and I managed to get my knife back. He was too horny to know that though. Long story short, when he was on me again, I cut his throat. It must've been his carotid artery because blood jetted several feet off to the side. He was easy to knock off at that point."

"Can you take us to that location?" Marcus asked.

"Sure," she answered hesitantly. "Whatever you need," she said, smiling at Darrick.

Kara jumped down off the table and fetched her gear. She also grabbed the sniper rifle that she'd hidden in the woods just after her confrontation with Tonya.

Tonya was watching and listening from the back door. She regretted that Kara hadn't been killed by the man at the dilapidated house and wasn't sure how things could be sustained at the status quo. So she waited to see how things would play out. There had never been a moment in her life when she'd felt so much malice. The entire experience was new to her. Adapting to this way of thinking would radically change her personality for the worse and possibly even speed up her physical deterioration. With all the added stress, she was feeling more and more under the weather. The pains were more frequent; some powerful, some not so much.

As she stood there in the kitchen, Darrick came into the house alone. He needed to grab his gear. When he met Tonya in the kitchen, he could see that she was troubled, but misunderstood what was troubling her. He grabbed a pack from the front room floor and met her again in the kitchen. This time he gave her a kiss on the lips.

"I love you," he said.

"I love you, too."

"Don't worry. I'll be fine. We're just going to see what we can find out about this guy who attacked Kara and –"

Tonya turned away from the conversation as soon as he said *Kara.* Darrick gently grabbed her by the jaw and turned her face up to meet his. "We need to identify the man. Only Marcus can do that. If he was one of them, then that means there's another one or two more of them out there."

"You can't keep leaving us alone like this. Remember the last time? And the time before that? Each time you run off, everything goes south."

Darrick looked behind her and saw Carissa standing there. It was a staunch reminder of what had happened to Jimmie.

"Marcus and Kara can go. Stay here with me," she pleaded.

"Alright," he said, conceding to his wife's plea. He dropped the pack and went to tell Marcus and Kara the decision.

"Hey, guys, I'm going to stay behind to watch over the fam'."

Kara was noticeably disturbed by the decision, but Marcus seemed okay with it. "No problem," Marcus replied.

"We'll be back before you know it," Kara said.

They stepped off.

Darrick stood in the back door and watched them as they walked away. His arms were folded and he seemed content with the final decision. Tonya walked up to him and hugged him, resting her head on his chest. Carissa saw the affection and instantly thought of Jimmie. She missed him dearly, but was over her anger toward Darrick for the way it had happened. She felt he was complicit, but not guilty.

As Tonya stood there with Darrick, hugging him, Andy entered the kitchen. "When can I go outside to play again?"

"Not yet, buddy. It's still not safe."

"It'll never be safe again, will it?"

The directness of children. Darrick knew it would never be safe again. Even if they succeeded and the Enclave never found the homestead, there would be other dangers. Other people that would come. The world was not the same. It was different. Hostile. Deadly.

"Mom's getting sicker," Andy said. He was more observant than he let on.

Darrick ignored the comment. Hoping not to add another set of issues to his plate. It was unavoidable. Inevitable. Tonya had a deadly cancer and it was living inside her. Growing every day. Eventually, they would have to face that set of fears. But for now, their minds were on the present.

The dilapidated shack

Kara led Marcus right up to the body of the man who attacked her. He was already covered in flies, and maggots were wriggling in the corners of his eyes. Each of them held their noses to shield against the horrific odor of decay.

"That's him. That's the guy. Do you recognize him?"

"I do. It's Frank Bentley."

"And?"

"And he's got a twin brother named Trent."

Mitchell Homestead

Knock, knock, knock.

Carissa, Tonya, and Darrick froze in their spots. The front door came alive with activity. They knew it wasn't Kara, because they had all agreed on a very specific *knock, knock, pause, knock* signal. "It could be Marcus," Darrick whispered. "We didn't share the knock with him."

"Kara would have told him before sending him back, right?" Carissa asked.

"I doubt she wants him dead. He can't run interference if he's not around to do it," Tonya said.

The comment went over Carissa's head, but Darrick knew what she was implying. Now wasn't the time to dispute affairs and old flings.

"Tonya, can you take Andy up to the hiding spot and help keep Dad quiet? He's starting to stir around up there."

"Yeah," she said, taking Andy by the hand and rushing him up the stairs.

Darrick looked at Carissa and said, "Can you hide behind the window and door with Dad's shotgun? I'll call on you when, and if, I need backup."

"You got it," she said, lifting the floorboard up to grab the shotgun from its hiding place.

Darrick reached into his pack and pulled out his pistol. He leaned the rifle against the trim of the door frame between him and Carissa. With the pistol in his right hand, he looked through the window of the door. It was a bearded man. Rough-looking.

Darrick wanted to go out through the back door and attempt an surprise attack, but in doing so, he could be falling into an ambush. The best course of action was the direct approach.

"What do you want?" Darrick shouted through the door and listened for a reply. The house could hear the conversation through the silence.

"I'm just looking for my brother. I wonder if you've seen him. Can you open the door so we can talk face-to-face?"

"I don't take kindly to strangers approaching my house, mister. I think it'd be best if you just go about your business."

The man seemed irritated about the response. Almost like he wasn't used to being spoken to in such a manner. "What do you do to people who encroach upon your property? You don't shoot 'em, do you?"

Darrick wanted to shoot the man right through the door, but he didn't know if there were more of them outside or if he was alone. It put a damper on his tactical responses. The longer the conversation went on, the more risk was being posed to his family and the homestead.

"I'm not telling you again, mister. This is your last chance. Get off my property."

"I'll take that as a *yes*. If I find out you shot my brother, there'll be hell to pay," the man said. The stranger started to back off the porch. "I'm just going to look around the yard to see if I can find some evidence that he was here. If you take a pop at me, your story will end here."

"Quick. Go look out the back window and tell me if you see anybody else. Pay special attention to the hiding spots. Remember, if you can see them, then they can see you. Be careful," Darrick said to Carissa.

She nodded, then ran for the kitchen with her shotgun in hand. She peered through the window. "I see nothing."

Darrick gave a quick look through the window at the front of the property while the man was walking away from him. "I don't see anything either. I'm going out."

"Be careful," Carissa said.

Darrick pulled the door open and ran out with his pistol drawn on the stranger. The stranger also had his weapon drawn up and pointed at Darrick.

"Easy there, fella. If you shoot me, this house will burn," the stranger said.

Darrick was still nervous that the man wasn't alone. He wasn't completely confident that the man was bluffing. After all, who could be so bold as to walk up to a man's house and make cold threats? Darrick nervously kept his pistol trained on the man.

"I didn't come here for a problem," the stranger said.

"Well, you found it," Darrick replied.

"There's no need to be uncivil about this."

Darrick did a visual scan of the rifle that was pointing at him. It was the same make and model as the sniper rifle that Kara had. Was it hers?

"Where'd you get that rifle, pal?"

"Why? Have you seen it before?" the man asked.

Darrick had unwittingly given the man a clue to the answer he was seeking. Darrick's slowness to reply validated something the man was considering.

"You know what? Never mind. I think I may have stumbled onto the wrong man's property."

There was yelling coming from inside the house. The stranger heard the commotion. "It sounds like you've got some domestic affairs to tend to. I'll be on my way."

"You're not going anywhere."

"You gonna stop me?"

Darrick and the stranger were having a standoff. It was a catch-22 for each of them. A checkmate.

Elder Mitchell came bursting through the front door. Tonya was immediately behind him. James fell down the stairs of the front porch. The stranger laughed. James wallowed around on the ground while

Darrick used his left hand to hold Tonya back. When Tonya looked at the man's face, she gasped.

The stranger caught it. "You've seen me before, haven't you?"

"That's him," she said in a soft voice. "That's the man who attacked Kara."

"Kara killed that man, Tonya," Darrick said.

"She's a liar. That's him. I'd recognize him in a lineup of a thousand men."

"I wish you wouldn't have said that, pretty thang," the stranger said. "I came here looking for my brother – my twin brother. Now I hear that he's dead. Kara, you said? Is that who killed 'im?"

"Don't answer him," Darrick said. Then he turned his attention back to the stranger. "I suppose that if you had any compadres, they'd be here already, eh?"

"I didn't say they were here, but they know I'm here. If I don't return –"

Crack! Crash!

The front room window shattered, and the man fell to the ground grabbing his chest. The rifle was also lying on the ground just out of reach. Darrick turned toward the sound. Carissa had taken the shot that Darrick wouldn't. From the cover of the front room, she'd seen the man and heard the conversation. She was prepared to take the risk. In any case, the man was now dying and he seemed to be alone. Tonya and Darrick stood silently still, but there was nothing. No movement, no shouting, no anything. Darrick looked back down at the man. He was slow to die, so Darrick took a knee on his neck, cutting off the man's flow of oxygen. Within a few seconds, the man was gone.

Darrick was zoned out. He watched the man as he stopped breathing, but his mind wasn't even on him. He was thinking about how much Carissa had changed. Not too long ago she had been berating him for talking about killing men. Darrick didn't know if he should be frightened or impressed.

"Darrick," Tonya said.

Snapping awake from his daydream, he looked at Tonya. "I want you to get Dad and Andy to Pontybridge at first light. If the Omen is heading west, then we'll head south and hopefully lose them."

"What about you?"

"I'll be with you unless Marcus and Kara aren't back by first light."

"And if they're not?"

"Then I'm going after them."

Tonya sighed.

"I know you're not fond of Kara, but she's a good person, and Marcus is my friend. He has some connections at Pontybridge. When you guys get there, drop his name and wait for us."

"Are you sure about this?"

"I'm not sure about anything anymore. The landscape has changed, and nothing is the way it should be. Survival changes people. It brings out the worst in humanity."

"What do you plan on doing in the meantime?"

"I have to get rid of the body," he answered, acknowledging the dead man on his front lawn.

Carissa stepped outside.

"Nice shot, by the way."

"Thanks. I just took the shot you wouldn't."

It was kind of a rub on Darrick's ego to have to hear that he had been outperformed by Carissa.

"Can you help me get Dad back in the house?" Darrick asked her.

"Sure," Carissa answered, assisting Tonya and Darrick in getting elder Mitchell to his feet.

James was able to walk on his own once he was up. Tonya took over and escorted him back into the house.

"I heard you talking to Tonya. You mentioned Pontybridge," Carissa said. "Jimmie always told me to avoid communities. He said there's always trouble to be found where people mass."

"I think he gave you some pretty sound advice, but I'm not one to discredit any advice Marcus might give me, either. I think if they stay mindful and observant, they'll be fine."

"I'm coming with you."

"I don't think that's a good idea," Darrick rapidly shot back.

"Well, you're not exactly known for your good judgment, so I'll consider your rebuke another bad choice."

Darrick turned to face Carissa. He wasn't looking for a confrontation, but she needed to hear what he had to say. "I need you to be with Tonya. She's sick, and it's getting worse every day."

"I've noticed."

"All the added drama with Kara and that isn't helping. I try to minimize where possible, but I don't think anything I do is going to help. She's an emotional roller coaster."

"I've noticed that, too. She won't be happy until Kara is gone."

"Do you think she left Kara to die?"

"Honestly?" Carissa asked, looking to the house to make sure Tonya wasn't listening. "I do. Hell has no fury like a woman scorned," she whispered.

"I don't know what to do."

"The way I see it, you can either tell her *things aren't working out* or Tonya will have to live with it."

"That's the problem, though. Tonya can't live with it. What if I'm killing her?"

"Then that's something you'll have to live with. Either way, Kara goes or Kara stays."

Carissa could see Darrick's conflict, but no advice would solve the problem. He was going to have to make a decision.

"Look," Carissa added, "I don't mean to be cold or indifferent, but Tonya's dying regardless of what you decide. Keeping Kara will speed things. If you only have so much time left with Tonya, why would you hang it out on a limb like a piñata?"

Darrick walked away from the conversation, tired of the topic. He fetched the wheelbarrow from the toolshed and brought it to the front, where Carissa helped him load the man's body onto it.

"Need any help digging the hole?" she asked.

"No, thanks. I got it."

"I'm going to join you anyway. I haven't visited Jimmie's grave since..."

"Okay," he answered.

The Glade

Several minutes later, Darrick was sweating over the shallow hole he'd dug for the man's body. Carissa kept him company as she sat across the way, close to Jimmie's grave. Darrick was beginning to notice that the graves were becoming shallower with each new hole he dug. He was over it.

"Four feet should do," he said, standing up to wipe his brow. "I'm tired of burying people. I'm done. This is my last." Darrick rolled the man over into his grave. This time, the man landed facedown. Darrick didn't care. He was jaded beyond repair. He spat on the man's body and shoveled the loose soil back into its spot.

Carissa stood up and walked over to Darrick. "Thank you for placing the marker on Jimmie's grave," she said, rubbing Darrick's arm. The bond they were forming was far more than it had been when he first arrived on their doorstep. Even Jimmie's death had caused a bit of discord between them, but she seemed to have moved on past that.

"It wasn't a problem. He's my brother. He deserves far better treatment than these guys are getting. I'm done burying people. They're like animals, so I'm going to treat them like animals."

The two of them left the cemetery together and shared memories of Jimmie as they went.

The dilapidated house

"I have what I need," Marcus said. "We need to be heading back to warn Mitchell. Trent's gotta be close to them by now. The Bentley brothers are trackers. I'm sure either you or Tonya led him straight back to the house. I'm surprised we didn't run into him on the way."

"I took another route back that night. That could explain why we didn't see him this trip. I was alone, so I took to the woods. If he followed that trail, then he'll be coming out on the west side of the house," Kara answered.

"Did you hear that?" Marcus said, holding his finger up to shush Kara.

"Hear what?"

"Shh, listen."

It was faint, but each of them could hear the sounds of a man yelling for help. It was coming from an easterly direction. Marcus climbed up the old television antenna that was attached to the house and looked out across the field. It was a man, and he was running from a crowd of men. "Hand me that scout rifle," he said.

Kara passed the long-range rifle to him.

He grabbed it and peered through the scope. "We need to get out of here, now," he said, climbing down.

"What is it? What did you see?"

"I think it's an Enclave war party, and they're chasing down a man tight with the leader of the group, which means he committed an offense against the Red Circle. He's marked for death, and we will be too if they see us."

When Marcus was on the ground, he gave the sniper rifle back to Kara. He took off running and she was close behind.

CAT'S OUT OF THE BAG

Mitchell Homestead

Darrick and Carissa exited the glade and immediately saw a plume of smoke rising into the air from behind the house. "Oh, God," Darrick said, scared for the lives of Tonya and Andy. He took off running as fast as he could. When he was close enough, he saw that the old barn was ablaze. He ran to the house and knocked on the door. Tonya opened it.

"Where's Andy?"

Tonya's lack of a rapid response let him know that she had no idea where he was.

"Tonya, where's Andy?"

"I don't know. I've been settling your dad down."

Darrick took off through the house, calling for Andy, but didn't get a response.

Carissa ran around to the back of the house and saw Andy standing near the old barn, which was blazing several yards into the air.

Inside the house, Darrick ran to the back door and opened it to see Carissa running up to Andy. She grabbed him by the hand to pull him away from the fire. When she did, she inadvertently grabbed a box of waterproof matches. She put them in her pocket and rushed Andy to safety. Darrick and Tonya were now outside and running toward Carissa and Andy.

"What are you doing?" Darrick yelled at Andy.

"Nothing," he yelled back.

"Why are you outside by yourself, and why were you so close to the fire?"

"I'm getting bored, so I –"

"He went out to play," Carissa interrupted. "He got bored, so he went out to play."

"How'd that fire start?" Darrick yelled.

"Darrick, it's summertime. Anything could've caught that old barn on fire," Carissa said, hiding Andy's secret from his father.

Darrick took several steps back and took in the enormity of it all. "That smoke is going to signal every survivor in our area that there's resources here," he said. "Pack your things. We need to be ready to move."

Carissa and Tonya whisked Andy away to the house, where they began throwing necessities into the bugout bags. Darrick took to the roof and watched things from a higher perspective. "I could really use that rifle Kara had," he said. As he scanned the area, he saw what looked like Kara and Marcus heading over the rolling hillside toward the house.

***

"That's not good," Marcus said to Kara. Each of them saw the smoke plume from their location. They were still several hundred yards away.

"That looks like Darrick's place," Kara added.

"I think you're right."

They had been watching the plume for some time, hoping that the fire wasn't at the homestead. The closer they got to it, the more they realized they had a problem on their hands.

Eventually, Marcus and Kara came running around the southeast side of the burning barn. The heat could easily be felt on their faces as they moved toward the house. Darrick met them in the backyard. Carissa and Tonya stayed indoors with Andy and James.

"Don't ask," Darrick said, anticipating Marcus's question. He pretty much knew that Andy had had something to do with it. "What did you find out?"

"Yeah, man. She killed an Enclave tracker. They usually move out in groups of two. It was a man by the name of Frank Bentley, and he has a twin brother who we think might be in the area," Marcus answered.

"Yeah, I think I might have buried him a few minutes ago," Darrick said.

"We can't stay here, Mitchell. We need to go."

"I think we can defend the place until the fire goes out. We'll be good after the smoke clears."

"That's not the problem," Kara said. "Marcus saw a war party, and they had to have seen the smoke by now."

"A war party?"

About the time Darrick asked the question, a man came running over one of the hills in the distance. He was yelling for help. A murder of crows circled above him.

Darrick grabbed Kara's sniper rifle from her hand and scoped the man out.

"It's a man by the name of Cornelius Woods. He's the right-hand man of the group in question," Marcus said to Darrick.

"Then he dies," Darrick responded, placing his finger on the trigger.

"He's already marked for death, Mitchell. Save your ammo."

"Explain," he said, pulling the rifle away from his shoulder.

"It's a long story, but if I were you, I'd start shooting at the ones coming up over that hill now."

Darrick's peripheral vision was restricted to the round confinement of the scope. When he heard Marcus's statement, he looked up over his scope, then back downrange, where he saw an enormous number of people running after the man. The sounds of gunfire could also be heard breaking the silence of the countryside. Darrick was in awe of the size of the incoming group of men. "Marcus, how's your aim?"

"Do you have a death wish? We need to run!"

Bang, Darrick's rifle blasted. He saw a man drop through his scope. The crowd of men who were chasing Cornelius stumbled over the man Darrick had shot. It slowed the crowd down, to a point, but Darrick's decision might have escalated the situation. There was a *crack* against the house behind where Darrick, Marcus, and Kara were standing. It startled them and they ducked about the same time the sound of the shot reached their ears.

Carissa and Tonya came running outside after hearing the loud *crack*.

"What was that?" Tonya asked.

"Get back in the house. It's not safe out here."

Tonya and Carissa looked past Darrick into the distance and saw the man and the crowd behind him.

Cornelius reached the protection of Darrick and Marcus. He tried to run past them, but Darrick swung his rifle like a baseball bat by the barrel and hit the man in the forehead.

Cornelius fell to the ground.

The women ran back inside.

Darrick aimed his rifle back toward the crowd and scoped out his next target.

Bang. The rifle went off again. Darrick dropped another man. The group was starting to scatter across the field, making it more difficult to select a target.

"They're going into the woods," Carissa said.

"We need to go, Mitchell," Marcus said.

"Don't you get it, Guy! There's nowhere to go!" Darrick shouted at his friend.

"Pontybridge. We can go to Pontybridge."

Crack, crack. The sounds of bullets were zinging past them. Marcus was taking cover behind the chicken coop, and Darrick was setting up on the outside table to get more accurate shots.

"Take Kara, Andy, Tonya, and Carissa and leave, Guy! Take care of them for me. I'm staying here. Who knows, if my luck holds out, maybe we'll be joining you."

"We? Who's left?" Marcus asked, not knowing about elder Mitchell.

"My dad. He's a dusty ol' fart and slow, too. He'll never make the evac."

Bang.

Darrick knocked off another trespasser.

"Can you please tell me before you pull the trigger? I'm going deaf."

"Tonya's sick, Guy. She has the cancer."

Marcus was shocked at the news. "How long?"

"Days. Weeks. We don't know without a physician. She's been unmedicated since the Pulse. I'm pulling."

Marcus covered his ears.

Bang.

"Thanks," he said, grabbing Darrick's usual rifle and aiming down the sights to select a target of his own.

Bang.

Marcus shot a man.

Just over their backs, the sound of breaking glass was heard from the house. Carissa was knocking out her bedroom window. She and Tonya were pointing their rifles out the upstairs windows.

Darrick and Marcus were looking back.

"What is this, the Alamo?" Marcus asked.

"I guess nobody's fleeing," Darrick said. "There's another option that doesn't involve me staying back with my old man."

"I'm listening."

"We can wait for night, then see if we can inch our way to Pontybridge. We can't move Dad by day. He's too cranky, too slow, and it's too risky. Not to mention the fact he's as stubborn as a mule."

Darrick was right. There was one way in and out of the Mitchell homestead. It was a one-and-a-half-mile-long dirt and gravel road that was surrounded on either side by woods. They would have to leave immediately if they had any hope at all of making it to the county road, which posed its own dangers. If they waited for dark, they ran the risk of being completely surrounded by the trespassers. The way Darrick saw it, waiting for darkness at least provided them with natural concealment. There was no guarantee either way.

"Okay then. Let's go with plan B. I like any plan that involves all of us leaving together and me keeping you around for a bit longer. We have some catching up to do."

***

Later that night

The darkness was smothering beneath a clouded sky. The moon gave no light that could be seen. Tonya fell asleep when things grew quiet outside. Andy was hiding in Carissa's bedroom closet. Carissa was awake with her rifle pointed out the window. Elder Mitchell was locked in his room. Carissa had used a rope to tether the door handle of his room to the hall closet door across from his room. Darrick and Marcus were downstairs with Kara and Cornelius, who was out on the floor. They were intently watching from the windows, which were all shot or busted out by now. The entire situation felt very surreal to all of them. Their future seemed grim at best, but none of them were willing to lie down and die without a fight. They had a solemn unspoken commitment that they were living and dying together. It was something the adults knew needed to be kept between themselves.

None of them knew that Andy was lying in the fetal position in the closet. He wanted to cry himself to sleep, but he was terrified. They were content knowing that he was hiding. In reality, he was awake and fearing for his mother's safety. He hadn't heard her voice for some time and was worried that she'd been shot and killed in the gunfight. Opening the door to check on her was on his mind, but it wasn't a chance he was willing to take.

Downstairs, Darrick and Marcus were discussing the next course of action.

"We'll need to go light," Darrick said. "We'll need a distraction out back. Whatever it is, we'll leave out the front door and head across the way to the glade where you met up with me. If we have time, we'll make gear adjustments and head for Pontybridge."

"What kind of distraction did you have in mind?"

A few minutes later

Cornelius was out cold when Marcus kicked him in the ribs. "Hey, Rev. Wake up!"

He attempted to stand, but failed. His wrists and ankles were tied together with 550 paracord. "What is this? What's happening?"

Cornelius couldn't see anything for the darkness, but the voice he heard was a familiar one. "Marcus, is that your voice I heard?"

"It is, and you're no longer welcome here," Marcus answered.

"We saved your life; now you're going to save ours," Darrick said.

"Something about the way you've got me tied up leads me to believe your intentions might be sinister," Cornelius said.

"Don't be silly," Marcus answered. "There's a mob of angry men on the front lawn, calling for your blood. We're going to give you a head start, though. When that back door opens, you're going to run as fast as you can."

"Please don't do this," Cornelius pleaded. "I can be of use to you, Marcus. I know things about the Enclave."

"There's nothing you know that I don't," Marcus answered.

Darrick was being quiet and taking in all the information.

"I know something you don't," Cornelius rebutted.

Marcus's attention was captured. "I'm listening."

Cornelius knew that if he shared what he knew about Denver, then he'd be of no further use to Marcus. He was now wondering what he might do and how he might use his knowledge as a bartering chip for his safety. He couldn't think of anything. He had one card to play, but it wasn't a winning hand. "Promise me that if I tell you, you won't send me out there?"

"No can do," Marcus said.

Darrick had no reason to hold his peace. He just didn't have a part to play at this stage of the plan. "What do you know?"

Cornelius heard the new voice. "Who's that?"

"My name's Darrick Mitchell. This is my property."

Cornelius considered the possibility that this might be the man the Enclave had been looking for. "Are you the man responsible for Denver's missing men?"

"Before I tell you anything or do anything for you, you're going to have to prove your value. Tell me what you know that Marcus doesn't."

Cornelius felt it was an even trade and considered it a deal. "Rueben and Denver are one and the same."

"What are you talking about?" Marcus said.

"Rueben is Denver. Denver is Rueben. He's a paranoid schizo who looks in a mirror for advice."

"How does that help things?" Darrick asked.

"Well, for one, you're not going to have to run deep into the company of the Enclave to take out Denver. Rueben will be here soon. If you take out Rueben, you've cut the head off the serpent."

"Darrick," Kara said, "don't do it. We need to stick to the plan."

"Who's that? What plan?" Cornelius asked.

Darrick sighed. He knew Kara was right. He'd made too many bad decisions that cost lives. He was going to stick with the group plan.

"I'm sorry, mister," Darrick said.

Kara cut Cornelius's ankles free. Marcus and Darrick grabbed him by the pants and armpits and lifted him to his feet. They walked him to the back door and quietly opened it.

Flick.

"What was that?" Cornelius asked. It was the very distinctive sound of a match strike. "What are you doing?" Cornelius's hands were still bound, so he was unable to reach back behind him to feel what was happening, but he saw a flickering light and realized he was being set up. He was shoved out the door.

"Run," Marcus said.

"Please reconsider," he begged.

Carissa was standing in the darkness. She put the box of matches back in her pocket. Tonya, James, Andy, and Kara positioned themselves near the front door. Tonya and Kara worked together to keep elder Mitchell silent. Tonya's hand was over his mouth. He was struggling with them, but lacked the strength to resist her. Carissa joined them, and they waited for the signal.

"I said RUN!" Marcus said, kicking Cornelius out onto the back porch. Darrick pulled his pistol and shot it into the ceiling. It startled Cornelius into compliance.

He ran out the back door as fast as he could; all the while a light flickered behind him. He heard what he thought was the sound of gunshots directly to his rear. He felt the sting of what he thought was bullet wounds. It didn't take but a couple of moments for him to realize the sound was firecrackers, not gunshots, and they were latched to his belt. It was at that point he knew he was a decoy. He saw the first flash of light from the tree line that signaled to him he was being shot at. He heard the sound, then felt a sting in his side and saw several more flashes of light and felt the stings that he recognized, undoubtedly, as impact wounds.

Everybody that was hiding outside with a view of the front yard left their positions to join in what sounded like a gunfight in the backyard. The blasts drowned out the silence. It was the signal Tonya, Carissa, and Kara were waiting for. The front door flew open and they ran out, struggling with elder Mitchell as they went. They were joined by Darrick and Marcus, Darrick being the one to pick his dad up into a bear hug to carry him out.

In the backyard, the string of firecrackers had all exploded and the gunshots were subsiding. Silence was regaining its dominance. Cornelius was lying on the ground with multiple bullet wounds, slowly dying from blood loss. He hadn't received a single fatal wound, but the sheer number of hits were enough to seal his fate. Several men were beginning to reveal themselves from their covered positions and making their approach toward the downed man. Others were keeping a watchful eye on the back door as they waited for more people to keep running out. It never happened.

"We got him," one of the men yelled. "It's Cornelius."

They gathered around him to confirm that they'd finished their task. Three or four men maintained security on the back of the house while the rest watched Cornelius breathe his last breath.

"There were more," a man said. "At least three or four more."

"Everybody, into the house. We need to make sure it's done," a man named Chad said, taking charge of the manhunt.

A large group of men entered the house. Within a few seconds, the verdict was announced.

"There's nobody here."

"Spread out and find them. They've got to be here somewhere."

"Who was covering the front door?" the self-appointed leader asked.

When nobody owned up to the question, he commanded them, saying, "They fled out the front door, you idiots. Go get them."

The group of men ran off across the front of the property and spread out to cover the vast amount of land. Several went down the graveled road, and others entered the woods.

***

Darrick and Marcus let the women, elder Mitchell, and Andy take the lead so that they could provide rear cover and fend off any would-be pursuers. They maintained a steady-paced trek through the woods that would take most of the night. They were well aware of the dangers and possible conflicts that could happen in a darkened forest, which was why Darrick and Marcus gave them such a substantial lead. It wasn't long after they had entered the woods that they started to hear the voices of men as they passed through.

The plan had been discussed before they ever left the house. They agreed to let the women take Andy and James ahead while Darrick and Marcus took out the trackers. Knives only was the agreement. Only as an absolute last resort were they to use guns.

Darrick and Marcus were about twenty feet apart when the first of the trackers came by. Darrick was wearing a white T-shirt that lit him up like a lightning bug against the dark forest. He used the trees as cover, being sure to keep a tight profile against an oak as a tracker walked by. Once he passed Darrick's position, Darrick quietly stepped out from behind the tree and knocked the man's rifle out of his hand and stabbed him in the throat. The wound was deep enough to open his windpipe so that the man couldn't yell. He didn't even fight. He used both of his hands to control the bleeding and dropped to his knees when they weakened from blood loss. Darrick knew it was fatal, so he moved on away from the man.

Marcus was wearing a blue-colored shirt, so it wasn't as visible as Darrick's. As long as he remained motionless, the trackers would just walk by him. When they did, he slit their throats from behind. Each one died the same way. They would drop their rifles and grab their throats.

There were several men who were well spread out. The darkness and the fact they were outnumbered made it an impossibility to take them all out. Everything seemed to be going fairly smoothly except for the fact some made it past Darrick and Marcus. It was Tonya's scream that alerted them to a problem with the plan.

Oh no, Darrick thought, hearing the scream.

Marcus heard it, too. They each moved as fast as they could through the forest. The cloud cover began to break up, revealing bits of moonlight. It was only a momentary relief that enabled them to pick up their pace. The moon vanished behind the clouds once again, and the first drops of rain were heard landing on the green canopy.

Darrick and Marcus weren't the only persons running through the forest. Tonya's scream was heard far and wide. It alerted the rest of the Enclave war party, who were also headed in the direction of the women, Andy, and elder Mitchell.

Darrick arrived first, having a head start over Marcus. When he arrived at the approximate location of the scream, he stopped running and stood silently listening. All he heard was Marcus running up from behind him.

"Marcus?" Darrick asked.

"Yeah, man. It's me. Where are they?" he whispered.

"Down here," Kara whispered.

Both Darrick and Marcus headed toward the sound of Kara's voice. As if on cue, the moon gave forth her light. Darrick saw Kara sitting in the woods, with Tonya resting on her back, her head being supported by Kara's knees. She was unconscious.

"What happened?" Darrick asked. Marcus made his way over to them.

"One of them grabbed her in a choke hold. I hit him on the back of the head with my rifle. He's over there," she said, pointing in the direction of the man's body.

Darrick went over to the man and cut his throat in his sleep. When the deed had been done, he returned to Kara, Tonya, and Marcus. "Where's Andy?"

"I don't know. He ran off, and Carissa chased him. Your dad made a break for it, too. I'm sorry. They went in opposite directions."

"Marcus," Darrick said, "can you head southeast? I'll head southwest."

"Sure," Marcus answered, heading off.

"Kara, can you get Tonya to Pontybridge? It's not safe here."

"Yeah," she answered.

"We'll catch up to you. Keep moving and don't stop."

"I will."

Darrick gave her a hug and ran off. He felt his way through the woods with the limited amount of light that was afforded to him. His knife was tightly gripped, so much so that he had to remind himself to relax on his squeeze. He pushed through the woods, moving as silently as he could, until he heard his dad's voice yelling through the darkness.

"Pudge? You're gonna get it, boy. You'd better show yourself or you'll get it twice as bad."

Darrick ran as fast as he could safely run toward his dad's voice.

"This is the last time I'm going to tell you!" James yelled under the cover of darkness.

Pinpointing his location was difficult. The woods were thick, and the land was hilly. His voice was being refracted by the terrain. In a panic to find his dad, Darrick bumped into Carissa, knocking her to the ground. In the confusion, Carissa pointed her rifle at Darrick and he pulled his knife on her. The confrontation only lasted a second before they realized who they were.

"Where's Andy?" Darrick asked.

"He's close. I was following his footsteps when I ran into you," she said, still breathing heavily from the chase.

Immediately, Darrick knew Andy was headed for his grandpa. "Oh no," he said, taking off again in the direction of his dad.

A few seconds later, Darrick was close enough to see his dad if lighting conditions were any better. The rain let up and it became deathly silent. All except elder Mitchell's yells. They were ear-piercingly loud. A ravine was all that separated Darrick from his dad. He would have descended it and crawled up the other side if not for the voices of two men he heard who were approaching his dad's side of the ravine. The canopy opened enough to let the moon's light shine on elder Mitchell's position. A bright green color in the tree above James gave away Andy's position.

He must've become frightened and hid from Dad, Darrick thought.

Elder Mitchell was confused. He thought he was looking for his son, but in truth he had seen Andy in the woods at night and was taking on his old role as authoritarian. Two armed men were making their way to where elder Mitchell was yelling.

When Andy saw his dad, he started to climb down the tree. Darrick was trying to persuade him to stay where he was, but he was watching his way down the tree instead of looking at his father.

Darrick's heart began to race. His mind was pumping with ideas on how to deal with the situation at hand. The men were aiming their rifles in the direction of James, but their view was obstructed by trees. They would stop, listen, and advance. Darrick decided to advance on his dad's position when the armed men advanced, hoping their footsteps would drown out the sounds of his.

When Darrick reached James and Andy, he grabbed Andy first and pulled him down into the ravine. Then he climbed back up the ravine and grabbed his dad, pulling him down. Elder Mitchell became so loud that he threatened to give away their position more than he had before. Darrick grabbed him by the mouth to try to silence him, but he fought with his hands and legs. Darrick had to make the ultimate decision of life and death. To leave things as they were, they would be heard, spotted, and shot. He looked at his son. Andy was terrified.

"Look away," he mouthed to his son.

Andy knew what had to be done, so he turned his head and covered his eyes.

Elder Mitchell was lying on Darrick, facing outward. He was fighting his son's attempts to keep him silent by trying to pull his hands off his mouth. Darrick knew he was making too much noise and there was nothing he could do except silence him. "Dad, please stop," he whispered with tears in his eyes. "Dad, please don't make me do this."

Elder Mitchell fought back the best he could, but he was feeble. That didn't stop him from kicking the earth beneath him and flailing his arms about. Darrick locked his dad's arms into position by putting them in the folds of his knees. With both of Darrick's hands now free, he was able to hold one hand over his dad's mouth and the other over his nose. Darrick closed his eyes, as if not seeing it would block the awful deed from his memory. James continued to kick violently. It was a sound that he was certain could be heard by the armed men who were already dangerously close to their hiding spot in the ravine.

Darrick cried. There was no other way. To save his son, he had to stop his dad from making so much noise. The men drew closer to the sounds. Closer yet.

"Do you hear that?" one of the men asked the other. They both stopped moving. "I don't hear the voice anymore."

"Me neither."

Both men were standing just over the top of Darrick, Andy, and James's now lifeless body, as Darrick held him tightly. Darrick was still crying, but he dared not make a sound. His facial expression was one of torment and great pain.

"Let's keep moving," the man said. With that, both men left the area and Darrick saved his son's life.

Enclave Camp
The next morning
August 18th

Rueben was sitting on the porch of the ranch house, picking the grime from beneath his fingernails with the file of his fingernail clippers. The wooden rocking chair had a slight squeak to it, but not enough to disturb his peace of mind. He was wondering why his war party was taking so long to return when word finally came to his ears.

"Boss," a man called out from the far side of the front yard.

Rueben looked up to see a sweaty man standing on the other side of the gate.

"They're back."

Rueben stood up and walked to the gate, where he met the men. "Roll call," he sounded off.

The men were tired from a long night of manhunting, fireworks, and gunfights. They came together in a loosely organized formation. Rueben looked at them once, then squinted his eyes. The numbers weren't right.

"Chad," Rueben called out. He knew Chad was a control freak who loved to take command of situations.

Chad was standing in formation when he heard his named called out. He looked at Rueben, who was pulling his handkerchief from his pocket to cover his nose and mouth. Chad was frozen with fear.

"Chad, come here."

Chad jumped out of formation. "I'm here, sir."

Rueben called out, "Red Circle," then pulled his pistol out. Once the group surrounded Rueben and Chad, Rueben pointed his pistol at him and shot him in the heart. He stood there and watched Rueben put his pistol away before he fell down and died.

"I see ten less of you than what I sent out yesterday. I can only assume they're dead. Blood in, blood out."

THE END OF BOOK ONE
COMING SOON: BOOK TWO, DEADFALL

BLOOD CORPS
PROLOGUE
Spring 2036
Evening Hours

Blake was running as fast as she could; her heart was pounding, her abdominal muscles were cramping, and she knew she couldn't slow her pace without the risk of consequence. She could smell the dank air that seemed to permeate the building and heard the sounds of crunching glass and debris beneath her feet as she ran.

The sun barely gave off its light as it dipped below the horizon, making it all the more difficult for Blake to see the obstacles before her. The adrenaline that coursed through her veins brought with it attuned hearing, dilated pupils, and speed. Not only was she acutely aware of her immediate environment and self-being, but she was also fixated on the chase.

The added adrenaline made it possible for her to keep up with the man she was chasing. She seemed to always be lagging just one room behind the man, who was also running as fast as he could. No sooner than he busted through one door into a strange room, he seemed to be charging into the next room. The man zigzagged around and over obstacles as he ran through what used to be personnel offices for the old factory building. Desks and cabinets seemed to pose him little to no difficulty. On some occasions he would grab a bookshelf or cabinet as he ran by it, only to throw it onto the floor behind him in a futile attempt to stop his armed pursuer. These obstacles had no real effect on Blake. She was a hardened active-duty Marine when the Flip went down nearly three years ago, so for her to jump over a cabinet or dash around a bookshelf was typical of the obstacle courses she was already accustomed to.

The man Blake was chasing was also a hardened combat veteran. He had been serving in the US Army as a computer programmer before being shipped to Iran to fight in the Jihadi Wars. He did that for a period of two years; then the Flip happened. Normally, he wouldn't run, but Blake's reputation preceded her. He was caught off guard when Blake took chase. Having set his rifle down to relieve his bladder, Blake had waited for the perfect moment to introduce herself.

One hour prior

"Ty Dodds," a feminine voice called out from behind him. He froze in his position and gave a moment to recollect the location of his rifle. He had set it against the wall some ten feet between him and the voice to his rear.

"It depends on who's asking," he replied.

"I was hoping you'd play nice, but since that's not an option, I'm going to have to get rough."

Ty looked over his shoulder and saw a redheaded lady with a small olive drab assault rig on her back. He gave her a quick study and could see that she was positioned with her left side towards him, with her right side facing away at a thirty-degree angle. The woman had a stiletto blade in her left hand and an empty sheath on her right leg. Her right hand was behind her and her feet were spread about shoulder width apart.

I can take her, he thought. *She's only armed with a knife.*

The redhead's name was Blake Cassidy. She had played an incremental, yet important role, in the final *Days of the Tyrant,* a term coined by the new American President, John James. She was well armed for this particular bounty. Unknown to Ty, she had an underarm holster that was hidden out of sight, fitted for a Glock model 22. That model shot a .40-caliber round and was paired with a fifteen-round magazine, which she had loaded with armor-piercing rounds. It was a heavy pistol, too heavy to leave holstered for a run of any length. Just above either ankle, she had an eleven-inch stiletto knife. On her right leg, she kept it sheathed on the outside of her pant leg; but on the left, she had one concealed beneath. Except, on this occasion, her pistol was tightly gripped in her right hand and concealed behind her back. The knife that was normally sheathed on her right leg was on display for Ty Dodds to see in her left hand.

"I know what you're thinking," Blake said.

"Do you, now?" he replied as he zipped his pants and turned to face her. His eyes were locked onto hers as he awaited her response. He was confident that he had the upper hand.

"Yep... You're thinking *I think I can take her. She's only armed with a stiletto.*"

"You're pretty good at that, miss..."

Ty purposefully didn't finish his statement. He was soliciting the woman for a name.

"Cassidy," she answered. "Blake Cassidy."

The man's face went flush. He could feel adrenaline surge through his veins. He knew the name. Every sketchy character in the land knew the name *Cassidy*.

The world had changed dramatically in the last three years. The changes were global and it meant a change in lifestyle for every living person. For Blake Cassidy, it meant taking up a job to earn a living. The year 2036 was like a hi-tech version of the Old West. Automobiles and horseback were two common modes of transportation. Paper money was a thing of the past. Currency was again being coined, as the original US Constitution had called for. To acquire a gold bit, one had to perform specific duties to earn one. The only other options were to steal or kill for gold bits. That was the route Ty Dodds chose; unfortunately for him, he was now the prey for one experienced bounty hunter.

At this point, Ty had two options. He was not always good at making wise decisions, but this choice could end badly no matter which decision he made. He had the option to reach for the gun, which was his first choice. He saw she was armed with a blade, but knew she was too sneaky to come at him with only a blade, which caused him to re-examine her posture and the placement of her right hand. He now knew she was most likely armed with a pistol. The knife was a mere distraction, most likely to taunt him into making a bold move that would heighten the sensation of the capture. He glanced at the rifle, which was close, but not close enough. Ty looked at Blake and back at the rifle. When he looked back at her the second time, she was smirking, as if to say *please go for the rifle.* When he didn't, Blake knew she wasn't going to get what she was hoping for.

"Fine," she said. "You're worth more alive. Back it up about three feet," she commanded, pulling her right hand out from behind her back to reveal her Glock. Ty backed up, raising his hands into the air, and Blake followed him in a forward motion until she came to his rifle. When she stooped down to pick it up, he ran into an open door that was near his position on the side of the factory.

"Wonderful," Blake said to herself as she gave chase.

It would be dark soon and Blake knew that if she couldn't catch Ty fast, he would most likely get away. She spent the next hour slowly searching the interior of the factory. He was nowhere to be found. Just as she was about to give up the search, a large grain hopper on wheels rolled towards her at a very fast rate of speed. She could see Ty looking around the hopper as he shoved it at her. She shot one round off, towards his leg, before she was smashed between the wall and the metallic bin. The round clearly missed, as the bin hit her arm, offsetting her aim. The man didn't stay to continue his assault, but instead ran towards the exit. She pushed the hopper away and gave chase.

A Few Minutes Later

Ty was cutting through offices and dashing over desks in a futile attempt to lose Blake, but she was tight on his trail. The exit was now a few feet away. The door was wide open and all Ty had to do was run a few more feet and he would again be outside, where he planned on performing a disappearing act. The sun had set and the outside world seemed to beckon to Ty. As he drew closer to the exit, the air freshened and he could feel himself drawn to it, like a moth is drawn to a flame.

Just as he met the threshold of the door in a dead sprint, Ty's face caught the back side of a shovel. A loud *clank* could clearly be heard by Blake, who was not twenty feet away from Ty's unconscious body. When she finally caught up, Tori Cunningham was standing over him, with shovel in hand.

"That counts as my catch," Blake said.

"How do you figure? You were in there for an hour with him. He nearly got away and probably would have if I hadn't been here."

"He's bleeding," Blake said, throwing her hands up into the air. "I never realized that when we started taking on bounty hunts, the rabbit hole would take us this deep. I mean, how much crazier is this going to get?"

"I don't know, but c'mon, you gotta admit… this was kind of a fun change of pace."

"Well, the bounty said *ALIVE*. He's bleeding, so…"

"Cute… since we're probably not going to collect on this one, I'd say we're good," Tori said, grabbing Ty's leg and giving him a pull. Blake grabbed the other leg and together they pulled him a block down the road, where they latched him onto a motorcycle and hog-tied him.

"Do you think he's gonna be upset when he wakes up on the back of a motorcycle that a woman is driving?" Tori asked.

"Probably so, but we'll fill him in when he wakes up."

Tori smiled back at Blake, and each of them rode off on their respective motorcycles, with Ty Dobbs in tow.

ACTS OF DEFIANCE
PROLOGUE

Over the past several decades, American tax dollars had been funding an ever-increasing amount of welfare programs. The programs continued to grow with the population, as did the tax dollar, so that they could be sustained.

By 2031, more than half of all Americans were dependent upon state and federal programs for food, water, housing, and utilities. With the ever-increasing number of people dependent upon these nanny programs, it became impossible for politicians who disagreed with them to win elections. Once more than half of all voters were dependent upon them, they became slaves to the party that promoted them.

With the southern border of the United States unsecure, wave after wave of undocumented aliens flooded into the system. These, too, became recipients of the welfare programs.

Mexicans, fleeing their homeland to find a means of survival, were not the only people crossing the border. For years, Islamic extremists, also known as *jihadists,* crossed with them.

These jihadists saw a weakness to exploit in the now fiscally destroyed America. Taking advantage of the opportunity, they waged their war on American soil, blending back into society after each attack. Political correctness became America's worst enemy; refusing refuge for undocumented aliens meant giving way to Islamic extremism.

With law enforcement's hands being tied from their efforts to profile, terrorism existed in and among the people of the United States.

When the people saw the government's inaction, they rose to the occasion to take matters into their own hands. They were quickly labeled as *domestic terrorists* by their own government and were soon a means to bring about more executive action by the President.

Cursive was removed from the educational curriculum, rendering most Americans with the inability to read the US Constitution, a document written in cursive. Legislation against gun manufacturers and ammunition manufacturers had put them out of business. The First Amendment freedom of expression was redefined as hate speech and punishable by law. Cameras and recording devices blanketed every city block, under the guise of protection, crippling the Fourth Amendment right to privacy.

With the Middle East Jihadist War in full swing, President Adalyn Baker called home America's armed forces. Street violence was escalating, joblessness was well over ninety percent, and Lady Liberty was taking her last breath.

Before the Flip
Murphysboro, Illinois, Friday, July 11, 2031

Stephen was sitting at the right end of the couch with his feet propped up on the coffee table, flipping through the channels with his TV remote in hand. Realizing his work boots were still on, he pulled his foot in to release the bootlaces, which had firmly been tied into place that morning. Years of tightly fastening his bootlaces around his ankles had caused a very distinct indentation around both of his legs, just above the ankles and under his calves. He was reminded of his service to country every time he took his work boots off. He was self-aware of the appearance and always felt insecure about the funny-looking formation. A shower was most definitely in order, but he had a tendency to relax for a few minutes before jumping into the tub.

"Steve!" his wife, Sam, said, walking into the front room as she covered her nose and mouth and added, "Don't you smell that?" referring to the pungent odor of Stephen's smelly work socks and boots that were still fresh from his hot summer factory job.

Stephen just smiled at her before pulling his socks off and wadding them each into a ball-shaped mass.

"Don't you dare!" she said, ducking back into the corridor and heading towards the kitchen. She made it two steps before she felt one of them hit her in the small of her back. "You're disgusting," she jokingly said, kicking it back into the front room.

Stephen feigned throwing the other sock at her. She kept flinching in anticipation of getting hit with another dirty sock. She wanted to run away, but was enjoying the playtime. Grossed out by the dirty sock she had kicked back into the front room, she cupped her nose shut and picked the sock up in a pinching motion with her index finger and thumb.

"If you come at me with that sock, you're going to get this one in your face," he warned.

Sam kept inching toward Stephen with her back toward him, hoping not to get a sock in the face. In one fluid motion, Stephen reached out to grab Sam from behind.

She screamed.

Stephen pulled her onto the couch with him. Instead of following through on his threat to shove a smelly sock in her face, he cuddled with her.

"What's for dinner, babe?" Stephen asked, making munching sounds in her ear.

"Potatoes au gratin."

"Argh, we had that yesterday," he said, letting go of her.

Sam rolled over on the couch to face Stephen. "I know, but they're not letting us pick out the goods anymore. We get whatever they give us."

"How did it even get this bad? I mean, I know how it did, but it's just stupid that we let it get this bad."

Sam stroked Stephen's hair. "Hon, you work fifty-six hours a week at the government's wheat plant, not counting your Guard duty, and we're barely making it, but we are. As long as we have each other, we're going to be okay."

Sam looked deep into Stephen's eyes and saw his concern. She loved rubbing her hands across his military-style high and tight. "I'm doing everything I can to get a job that can help pitch in around here."

Stephen pulled Sam in close to his chest and nestled his face in her hair. "You're doing everything I need from you already. If we can't make it off of two government incomes, we probably won't be able to make it off of three."

Stephen enjoyed having Sam at home as a housewife, but never restricted her to that lifestyle. But he always made it known to her that it was preferred over her leaving home to work. Their daughter, Evan, was in second grade, and Stephen felt it was difficult enough scouring through her homework to make sure the government-provided propaganda wasn't going against their family values. With Sam working, it would mean both Stephen and Sam would be too tired to assume the responsibility of proofing the homework.

"So how did it go down today at the food lines?" Stephen asked.

"Same as usual, only this time, they handed me yesterday's dinner. Actually, they didn't have the usual *assembly-line* structure they used to have when they bagged our goods."

"If I wasn't working for the Guard, we probably wouldn't be eating at all."

"Hon, your commitment to God and country paid off. We are much better off than they are," Sam said, raising the blinds to let the hot summer sun flood into the room.

Standing outside, mobs of people assembled themselves outside of the government buildings, hoping to fill their empty bags with food handouts. Many of them were holding signs expressing what used to be a protected first amendment freedom of expression. Those rights had been unconstitutionally abolished when crowds were randomly being arrested under the guise of unrest.

Stephen and Sam were looking out of the window when several black armored government trucks pulled in. The mobs of people broke up, many of them disappearing between the buildings, but others were caught by the police and handcuffed; each of them were forced into the back of windowless trucks, where they were whisked away.

"They were peacefully protesting," he said with frustration apparent in his voice.

"Honestly, I can't remember a time when the police weren't breaking up peaceful protests," she countered.

"I do. It was before the Muslims got their jihad. Every time a crowd grew large enough to draw media attention, some *extremist* would blow himself up or send a brainwashed Muslimah to do the dirty work."

"I can't remember the last time I saw any media coverage on it."

"That's because the government's been in bed with the media since the Clintons."

Their conversation was interrupted when the news channel's coverage of the Jihadist War switched from an imbedded reporter in Iran to a cameraman's view of a podium. Centered on the podium was the Seal of the President of the United States. Sam saw it first. Tapping Stephen on the shoulder, she said, "Hon, look."

"What now, more executive orders?"

"Shhh," Sam said, interrupting Stephen. "President Baker's coming out."

It wasn't like Sam to *shush* Stephen. She was a very timid wife, despite her fun-natured personality. It took Stephen by surprise when it happened. He was still tired from his long shift, so he snapped back uncharacteristically.

"Don't shush me."

Sam just looked at him, surprised that he had snapped back at her.

"I'm sorry," he said, realizing that the punishment didn't fit the crime.

"It's okay."

They both turned their attention back to the television, where Adalyn Baker was now standing at the President's podium. Spanning the breadth of the bottom of the screen were the words *STATE OF THE UNION ADDRESS*.

> "People of the United States, last year we experienced an economic collapse, which was the result of the Republicans' *war on terror*, a war which

was drummed up by hypotheticals and scare tactics used by their right-wing conspirators. The country was still in a recession from the previous two decades of war. It was at this time I pulled the majority of our resources out of the Middle East conflicts and turned our budget towards more important issues, those being the welfare programs which are currently sustaining over ninety percent of you. Unfortunately, it was too little, too late. Now, as we look down the precipice of another collapse, the collapse of an antiquated form of democracy, we must embrace a new set of truths: that we, as a society, must take from each according to his abilities, and give to each according to his needs.

"Several months ago, I signed an executive order authorizing the Federal Emergency Management Agency to enforce a mandated identification system. This system has been in use for several years now with our military men and women. The Radio Frequency Identification system allows for quick, manageable, and sustainable means to make transactions in a fair and meaningful way that does not exclude the needy or favor the wealthy. With this program in place, every American will be equal and class warfare will become a thing of the past. As a part of this executive order, thousands of RFID stations have been set up in virtually every jurisdiction on the county level. In order for this program to work, America needs you to play your part. Every American will be required to report to their county authority to receive a subdermal implant, free of charge. The implant is tiny, the size of a rice grain, and will enable you to buy, sell, and trade. Together with our

European allies, we are joining economies and laying the groundwork for a one-world currency, and ultimately, a one-world economy. In our nation's history, never have we seen such a bright future. France, Italy, China, Japan, Germany, Russia, and Australia have already begun the implementation of this program, and have taken the lead in a forward direction.

"Unfortunately, we are expecting to be met with resistance right here in the United States. No doubt, there will be extremists on the right that will call this *tyranny* or some other derogatory and antiquated term. However, you must keep in mind that these domestic disturbance instigators are in the minority and are of no relevance. This program will succeed because it is the will of the people, which brings me to my next point.

"Due to the rise in numbers of domestic terrorists, otherwise known as *militias*, and the escalation of unfortunate events, which occur at their every appearance, I am reluctant but forced to invoke several existing executive orders. We have received word of several instances of insurrection against the current elected government. I feel that our national security is at risk and that these minority groups pose a substantial risk to vital resources. Therefore, I am invoking Executive Order 10997, which will provide the people with government-controlled resources, such as petroleum products, electricity, etc. To prevent our farmers from falling victim to these groups, I am invoking Executive Order 10998, to provide government oversight to all agricultural assets. In order to assure that these individuals do not interfere with the application of the RFID program, I am invoking Executive Orders 10999 and 13603, suspending all unauthorized transportation and providing government-supplied water. The government will be the sole distributor of all materials until I deem it safe to lift the government seizures. This will ensure unaltered and continued continuity of care to all citizens under my care.

"It has been determined that right-wing dissenters are responsible for the explosions occurring at peaceful protest sites and political rallies. This is why I suspended the First Amendment. It was not in objection to dissenting views, but rather the fact that these militia groups are showing up with assault weapons, and this is usually followed up with fatal and catastrophic events. For some time now, legislation has been insufficient in the control of these individuals finding ways to arm themselves and taking up insurrection against their government. Therefore, I am indefinitely declaring a state of martial law for the purpose of securing our borders against the threat of these domestic terrorists. Until these executive orders are lifted, a mandated curfew will be in effect starting thirty minutes after sunset and lasting until thirty minutes prior to sunrise on a daily basis. Travel chits will be issued by your local law enforcement agency so that those authorized to travel may do so.

"The United Nations have pledged their support and resources to aid us in these coming weeks. We have taken the lead in withdrawing our troops from the war in the Middle East. Our friends in Europe, Asia, and Africa will begin the withdrawal of their forces in the coming weeks. Russia will most likely continue on with their efforts in the Middle East conflicts, but the United States have played their part and are now tending to more pressing matters here at home.

"Effective immediately, congressional powers are revoked indefinitely. The legislative and judicial branches will have no authority until the domestic threat has been abated. The patriot movement will be stopped. Our resolve to pursue national security has never been stronger. Thank you."

TYRANT
BOOK ONE THE RISE
PROLOGUE AND CHAPTER I
PROLOGUE

By the year 2025, the United States had run its economy into bankruptcy. For years, fiscally conservative Republicans and Democrats complained about the unsustainable deficits. The liberal news media had stopped covering issues regarding the US economy, choosing instead to cover the brutalities of war and police use of force. Censorship against US citizens was the norm and any kind of media coverage on the government was the exception. The Federal Communications Commission controlled the internet, congressional legislation forced local business to pay ever-increasing minimum wages, and the government was providing healthcare and other amenities at the expense of private and corporate infrastructure. Taxation was no longer meeting the requirements necessary to sustain the status quo.

By 2030, local business could not afford to pay its employees. The US dollar was almost worthless and the government could no longer sustain public welfare. The internet was inaccessible, joblessness was above ninety percent, it was illegal to gather in public groups, and free speech was redefined.

In 2031, the President of the United States, seeing she could no longer control the angry American mobs or provide for the starving masses, declared martial law, invoking Executive Orders 10998, 10999, and 13603, seizing all public modes of transportation, and declaring eminent domain over all farmland, oil fields and refineries, water supplies, and food-processing plants. No one was allowed to store food, hoard water, or own energy sources.

Shortly thereafter, Executive Orders 10995 and 10997 went into effect, seizing all media, including radio, TV, telephones, satellite communications, newspapers, and lastly, electricity. In a matter of months, there was a complete revocation of constitutional law. It was no longer safe to travel, trade, or offer opinionated speech. America went black.

CHAPTER I
Southern Illinois, October 22, 2032

Jessica's morning started like any other morning. Southern Illinois in the fall is the place to be for anybody that loves stormy weather and the sound of thunder as lightning flashes through the sky. It wasn't exactly her dream home, but it would do for the time being. Her shoddy, half-sunk, rusty barge stank of fish and dirty river water, but it was away from the ensuing chaos in the town up the hill. The Chester Police refused to work for free, and the Randolph County Sheriff's Office didn't agree with the unconstitutional control of the US citizenry. Essentially, all rural areas of the United States were left to their own devices, so long as it didn't interfere with the president's hold on executive power.

Before the "Flip," a term used to describe the day the first executive order was declared, Jess was a full-time correctional officer and a part-time police officer. She was only thirty-two, but had twelve years vested into the state as a correctional officer, and six years in law enforcement.

When the Flip went down, southern Illinois was already in disarray and any person with a keen eye could see it coming. At first, Jess was most worried about all the Southern rednecks as food sources began to dwindle. Her first instinct was to be wary of them because she feared they would use those arms to secure food in unlawful ways. After the Flip, she saw these rednecks more frequently in the woods. That was how they secured their family's food sources. As she thought on it, she came to understand that these people had been armed for years and were perfect law-abiding citizens.

Early on, after the Flip, she had found herself having to readjust to new norms and force herself to rethink and retrain her mind. The old ways were gone and a new era required new thinking. For Jess, this meant watching the new behaviors of the people she had previously sworn an oath to protect through the upholding of the Constitution of the United States. She had sworn the oath on two separate occasions: first when she was hired on as a CO, and the second time when she was hired by the city of Chester to work as a cop.

On this particular morning, Jess had an inkling to walk up the city steps, from the shore of the river to the Randolph County Courthouse, in an effort to acquire a copy of the US Constitution. To do so would mean leaving the cover and security of her camp and exposing herself to the hazards of the world above. Jess felt that she was up to the task, so she donned her service pistol, which was a Glock 22 chambered in .40 caliber, and secured it in the small of her back, where it was snugly fitted against her frame, concealed in a padded holster. She also had an AR-15 in .223 with a 5.56 chamber. Its sixteen-inch barrel provided for excellent tactical use when combined with its collapsible stock, but did not have much accuracy beyond three hundred yards. She had previously taken the scope off of it because it only bumped around the reticles and became more of a nuisance than anything. Besides, she was an accurate shot with her iron sights and felt perfectly capable without a scope.

Jess slung the rifle across her back. She was wearing khaki-colored tactical BDU pants with cargo pockets and a bullet-resistant vest under a khaki-colored long-sleeved tactical shirt. On the sleeves and shoulders of her shirt, you could see the outline of where her police patches used to be. After the Flip, she knew what was next, so she tore them off. Jess wanted no association with the tyranny of the federal government. Whether it was true or not, she believed the people would make the police out to be the face of government. Jess was first and foremost an American. She wanted to move up that hill and secure a copy of her country's founding document, so with a deep breath and a quiet sigh, she headed up the city steps towards the courthouse.

Upon approaching the back side of the courthouse, where the Sheriff's Department was attached, Jess could see that the Sheriff's Department's vehicles had broken windows and the body of the vehicles were spray-painted with various graffiti and vulgar threats about law and order. She noticed the sally port door was still in place, but the windows to the Sheriff's Department were broken and the building itself was exposed to the elements. Jess removed her AR from where it was slung across her back and brought it to the ready as she carefully and cautiously approached the entrance to the apparently abandoned building. The inside appeared to be ransacked. There wasn't any sign of life from what she could tell. It wasn't but a moment of standing still and listening before Jess heard a noise coming from the jail area. It dawned on Jess that there might yet be prisoners, either loose or jailed, in the building.

The jail gate was open and she took her time to listen a moment longer before maneuvering toward the sound. What she heard was eerie and sent chills down her spine. It was the sound of feeding carnivores, crunching bone, and tearing meat. Jess knew that bobcats had made a comeback in southern Illinois, but reasoned that what she was hearing wasn't exclusive to bobcats. There were too many scuffling sounds to be a bobcat. Bobcats are solitary predators and this sound was more like a sound of pack animals. The sound was steady, so she moved slowly toward the dispatch office and turned left towards the jail, her weapon at the ready.

NO LIGHT BEYOND
Prologue
Two Years Earlier

"Lydia!" Mason cried out as he pushed through the debris of his upper-level apartment. "Lydia! Where are you?" Mason's heart was pounding as he kicked chunks of wall that were blocking his path out of the way. He called her name over and over again, but there was no response. Just outside, at ground level, screams could be heard at random intervals, almost always followed immediately by the sound of a gunshot blast.

The electricity that normally hummed through the walls and lit the nighttime sky was gone; the sounds of vehicles in the streets were no more. The only thing that lit the heavens was the moon, and it was rapidly disappearing in a gray-colored haze. Mason never wanted to raise his nine-year-old daughter in the Windy City. He knew crime rates were notoriously high, but figured violence was more prone to be located in the impoverished sections of the inner city, so he rented them a fancy, but affordable apartment away from the violence. He was the only male office associate in his office, which was a far cry from his training in the military and work as a mercenary in the war. He never allowed that to deter him because he took the job for his precious daughter, Lydia. Nothing else mattered to him.

"Lydia? Are you here?" he yelled into the darkness. "Tamara?" he called out, hoping that maybe his babysitter was still in the apartment, but she didn't answer either. Mason realized he was now searching the dark apartment in vain. He felt his way along the walls using nothing but memory and touch to steer him to the front door and into the main hallway. As he moved along, he heard a loud gunshot in the next apartment. After that, the scurry of what sounded like two or three men came bustling out the door. The voices were African-American males, and one of them said, "Hurry, grab the girl and let's get outta here."

Mason knew the neighbor and all of his comings and goings. He was a friendly old widower that used to help keep an eye on the place in his absence, and he didn't have a girl. None of those men belonged in that apartment, and Mason feared the worst. It was that very fear that gripped his heart. He was unarmed but didn't hesitate to give another shout for his daughter and push his way through the darkness towards the neighbor's door.

"Lydia," he shouted. He imagined the worst-case scenario and figured those men had just killed his neighbor and probably had his daughter in tow, provided the information at hand. When he had made his way back out into the darkened hallway, he heard two more shots coming from farther down the hallway. Mason called out for his daughter again, but there was no answer. After a brief moment, Mason began heading down the hallway, where he stopped to listen. It was there he heard Lydia's voice for the last time. "Please don't hurt me. Let me go."

Mason panicked and ran down the hallway, where he collided into men with flashlights. One of them pointed the light into Mason's eyes.

"Hey," he shouted to the men, but he could not see them for the brightness of the light. Mason immediately grabbed the man's hand that was carrying the flashlight and pulled him off balance. He followed up by raising his knee as high as he could and brought it down onto the stranger's leg, at the joint, dislocating the man's knee from the side.

"Daddy, help," Lydia cried out.

The next thing Mason saw was bright flashes of light accompanied by the deafening sounds of three or four bullets being shot in his direction.

"C'mon, Smoka," one of the men said. "Let's get outta here." The man known as "Smoka" stopped shooting, and one of the other men grabbed the man with a broken leg and helped him to his feet.

The men continued towards the emergency exit, leaving Mason alone, gripping his abdomen as the men carried off his precious daughter. He had a burning sensation in his stomach, and he could feel the warmth of his own blood on his hand. He made his way to the exit, where he saw the flashlight go, and started his descent down the stairs. He could hear the men far ahead of him, pounding their way down the steps. The metallic handrails carried a *ting* sound for long distances, as did the distinctive squeaky sole on the bottom of one of the men's shoes.

Mason could feel his legs were getting weak as he moved along. He had an intense will to soldier on toward the exit of the building.

Mason finally exited the building and fell to the ground.

"Lydia," he shouted over and over again.

"Lydia," he said in a softer tone. His strength was waning, and with it went the power to call for his daughter. Mason looked up at the moon and watched it as her glory faded into blackness. The gray haze covered the night sky. With his daughter gone, he surmised that his life was about to end. He considered the violence that covered the streets; wolves prowling the streets with flashlights and firearms killing innocent men and women for their belongings. There was little hope that he would reach Lydia alive.

Mason lay down on his side and rested his head on his arm and waited for his sight to go dim. Across the street sat a blind homeless man he had seen a hundred times before. The streets were running wild with violent activity and chaos, but that old man was as calm as the morning sea. The cardboard sign he was holding read "Isaiah 26:19." Mason always told himself he would look it up someday, but he never did.

A moment later, Mason could hear a person run up on him and grab him by his arm. The watch that was on his wrist was a Walmart purchase, but the thief didn't know what he was taking. Mason felt the person's hand patting up and down his body. It made its way down to his side and reached into his back pocket to steal his wallet, but he didn't even care. The person left, and the next thing Mason knew, he was being dragged down the sidewalk by his legs.

As he helplessly gave way to whatever fate would befall him, he looked out into the ensuing chaos and saw another man running at him with a baseball bat. Whoever was pulling Mason by the leg dropped it to take on the bat-wielding man, but he wasn't alone. He had a friend come running up behind him. "That's him, Smoka. Look at the gunshot wounds."

Smoka hit the man with the bat a few times while the second assailant began kicking Mason in the ribs and abdomen. Mason was so out of it, all he could do was watch as his own consciousness faded in and out. His eyes were blurry, and he couldn't make out the details of the men's faces.

When Smoka was done beating the mystery man, he turned to face Mason. "You shouldn't have interfered in my business." Then he drew the ball bat over his head and brought it down across Mason's forehead.

OATH TAKERS

ON OUR FORM OF GOVERNMENT

The Constitution, the Bill of Rights, and the Declaration of Independence hang above my fireplace. I also keep a copy of these articles in my prep bag. They are very dear to me. Not only will I die for their preservation, but I will fight with every fiber in my being to ensure my children and your children grow up with individual freedoms. Not the freedoms elected to them by the majority, or a dictator, of sorts, but individual sovereign freedoms. This is where one may be confused regarding the current status of the United States.

Our country is currently running as a democracy. It is not written into the Constitution as such. This country was forged to be a *republic*. Even our Pledge of Allegiance is *"to the Republic for which it stands"* (referring to the symbol of the US flag). In a republic, the individual American is sovereign to his/her own rights. Rights are vested with each and every individual American, equally. There should be no *democracy* among the citizens of the United States. In a *democracy*, the rights are vested in the majority. Where the majority dictate, the rights of the individuals in the minority do not apply. In a democracy, when the majority says "thus and such shall be your rights," then those are the rights given to you.

Our Constitution contains a Bill of Rights built into it to insure an everlasting individual freedom. This is why it's so important to protect, defend, and preserve the Constitution of the United States. I do not pretend to be a Constitutional professor. I'm not even a Constitutional senior lecturer; history shows that these titles don't mean too much when a country is being managed by educated derelicts with such abbreviations following their names. That's the beauty of the Constitution. It wasn't written by the educated for the educated. It was written by patriots that dreamed about a country where every person could be free from an overreaching government, where the government would be *the people.* It was written by a thirty-three-year-old planter by the name of Thomas Jefferson. The context of the Constitution is in the history of its creation. It was affirmed and voted into writ by a people fresh from the bonds of tyranny. They saw how a king could become corrupted by power and they watched as it happened.

Though years of intercession to the king went unanswered, it became necessary to fight and die for a great cause. The Constitution was written to permanently eradicate tyranny and to give power to the people of its citizenry. It was written in a time when government was not made up of *the people*, but rather a government unto itself that was made up of people, but not *for the people* or *by the people*. Therein lay the corruptibility of the government. It was through this avenue that the people of the American colonies became victims of their government, and therein lay the reasons the very words were penned:

"When in the Course of human events, it becomes necessary for one people to dissolve the political bands which have connected them with another, and to assume among the powers of the earth, the separate and equal station to which the Laws of Nature and of Nature's God entitle them, a decent respect to the opinions of mankind requires that they should declare the causes which impel them to the separation." —*The Declaration of Independence, July 4th, 1776*

The oath you swore was to the Constitution. It was not to an evolving form of government. Over the past several decades, a representative democracy has been the norm, but it was not so in the beginning. One of the greatest concerns during the early convention meetings was securing individual freedoms. Therein is the importance of the Bill of Rights. There will be more on that later, but our oaths are to those laws of the Constitution that give rights to sovereign Americans. As oath takers, your job is to ensure that these rights are kept within the confines of the Constitution and not usurping it. It is to make sure no person, foreign or domestic, tramples them. This defense mechanism was built into the Constitution.

ABOUT THE AUTHOR

L. Douglas Hogan is a USMC veteran with over twenty years in public service. Among these are three years as a Marine Corps antitank infantryman, one year as a Marine Corps Marksmanship Instructor, ten years as a part-time police officer, and twenty years working in state government, doing security work and supervision. He has been married over twenty-five years, has two children, and is faithful to his church, where he resides in southern Illinois.